## "That can't happen! I can't be in that kind of danger."

Weston tried to keep his voice as calm as possible. Hard to do, though, with the emotions swirling like a tornado inside him. "I'm sorry. If there was another way to stop him, then I wouldn't have come here. I know I don't have a right to ask, but I need your help."

"I can't."

"You can't? You must want this killer off the street. It's the only way you'll ever be truly safe."

Addie opened her mouth. Closed it. And she stared at him. "I'd planned on telling you. Not like this."

There was a new emotion in her voice and on her face. One that Weston couldn't quite put his finger on. "Tell me what?" he asked.

She dragged in a long breath and straightened her shoulders. "I can't be bait for the Moonlight Strangler because I can't risk being hurt." Addie took another deep breath. "I'm three months pregnant. And the baby is *yours*."

# LONE WOLF LAWMAN

USA TODAY Bestselling Author

DELORES FOSSEN

Recycling programs for this product may not exist in your area.

ISBN-13: 978-0-373-74920-1

Lone Wolf Lawman



This edition published by arrangement with Harlequin Books S.A.

For questions and comments about the quality of this book, please contact us at CustomerService@Harlequin.com.

Printed in U.S.A.

**Delores Fossen**, a *USA TODAY* bestselling author, has sold over fifty novels with millions of copies of her books in print worldwide. She's received the Booksellers' Best Award and the RT Reviewers' Choice Best Book Award. She was also a finalist for a prestigious RITA® Award. You can contact the author through her webpage at dfossen.net.

**Books by Delores Fossen**

**Harlequin Intrigue**

***Appaloosa Pass Ranch***

*Lone Wolf Lawman*

***Sweetwater Ranch***

*Maverick Sheriff*
*Cowboy Behind the Badge*
*Rustling Up Trouble*
*Kidnapping in Kendall County*
*The Deputy's Redemption*
*Reining in Justice*
*Surrendering to the Sheriff*
*A Lawman's Justice*

***The Lawmen of Silver Creek Ranch***

*Grayson*
*Dade*
*Nate*
*Kade*
*Gage*
*Mason*
*Josh*
*Sawyer*

Visit the Author Profile page
at Harlequin.com for more titles.

## CAST OF CHARACTERS

***Weston Cade***—A Texas Ranger with a dark past and a personal vendetta against a vicious serial killer dubbed the Moonlight Strangler. Weston's hunger for justice puts him on a collision course with rancher Addie Crockett, who has close, personal ties to the killer.

***Addie Crockett***—Adopted by a loving family when she was a toddler, Addie's world is shattered when she learns she's the biological daughter of the Moonlight Strangler. Reeling from the news, she finds herself in Weston's arms before she realizes he's not who he's claiming to be. But Addie has some startling news of her own to deliver to the hot cowboy cop.

***The Moonlight Strangler***—He's murdered at least twenty women, and despite their blood ties, he could want Addie for his next victim.

***Jericho Crockett***—Addie's adopted brother and the sheriff of Appaloosa Pass. He has one goal—to protect his sister—and no one had better get in his way, including Weston.

***Alton Boggs***—A wealthy politician who has his own personal connection to the Moonlight Strangler.

***Ira Canales***—Boggs's ruthless campaign manager who'd do anything to see his candidate win.

***Lonny Ogden***—A troubled young man. Is he working for the Moonlight Strangler? Or does he have his own agenda?

***Daisy Vogel***—A mystery woman from Addie's childhood. She could be the key to uncovering some deadly secrets.

# *Chapter One*

Addie Crockett heard the footsteps behind her a split second too late.

Before she could even turn around and see who was in the hall outside her home office, someone grabbed her.

She managed a strangled sound, barely. But the person slapped a hand over her mouth to muffle the scream that bubbled up in her throat.

Oh, mercy.

What was going on?

This was obviously some kind of attack, but Addie wouldn't just let this person hurt her. Or worse. She rammed her elbow into her attacker's stomach, but it did nothing to break the grip he had on her.

"Stop," he snapped. "I won't hurt you."

Addie wasn't taking his word for it. She turned, using his own grip to shove him against the wall and into an angel Christmas wreath. The painted wooden angels went flying. But not the man.

Addie tried to get his hand off her mouth so she could call out for help. Then she remembered her brothers weren't at the ranch. Two were still at work, and the other was Christmas shopping in San Antonio. Only her mother was inside the house, and she had a sprained ankle. Addie didn't want her mother to come hobbling into the middle of this.

Whatever *this* was.

"Stop," he repeated when she kept struggling. His voice was a hoarse whisper, and he dragged her from the hall into her office.

Addie gave him another jab of her elbow and would have delivered a third one if the man hadn't cursed. She hadn't recognized his order for her to stop, but she certainly recognized his voice now.

Wes Martin.

The relief collided with the slam of adrenaline, and it took Addie a moment to force herself to stop fighting so she could turn around and face him. Even though the sun was already close to setting and the lights weren't on in her office, there was enough illumination from the hall to see his black hair. His face. His eyes.

Yes, it was Wes all right.

The relief she'd felt didn't last long at all.

"What are you doing here?" Addie demanded. "And how'd you get in the house?" Those were only the first of many questions, and how much else she told him depended on what he had to say in the next couple of seconds.

He didn't jump to start those answers. Wes stood there staring at her as if she were a stranger. Well, she wasn't. And he knew that better than anyone. He'd seen every last inch of her.

Ditto for her seeing every last inch of him.

And despite the fact that it was the last thing Addie wanted in her head at this moment, the memories came of Wes naked and of her in his arms. Thankfully, he wasn't naked now. He was wearing jeans, a button-up shirt and a tan cowboy hat.

But there was something different about this cowboy outfit.

Beneath his jacket, he was wearing a waist holster and a gun.

"I came in through the side door." He tipped his head toward the hall. "It wasn't locked."

That wasn't unusual. Because the ranch hands—and the family—were often coming and going. They rarely locked up the house until bedtime. Even then, that was hit-or-miss since security wasn't usually an issue.

Until now, that was.

"I didn't see your car," she said, and since she'd just come in from the main barn, Addie would have seen any unfamiliar vehicles in the circular driveway in front of the house.

"I parked just off the main road and walked up. I'm sorry," he added, following her gaze to his gun. "But I had to come."

That didn't answer her other question as to why he was there, and Addie wasn't sure if she just wanted to send him packing or try to figure out what the heck was going on.

She went with the first option.

Wes had crushed her heart six ways to Sunday, and there was no need for her to give him another chance to hurt her again.

"You're leaving," Addie insisted, and she turned around to head to the hall so she could usher him right back out the side door.

She didn't get far because he took hold of her arm again. Not the tight grip he'd had before, but it was enough to keep her in place. And enough to rile her even more. "Let go of me."

"I can't." Wes opened his mouth, but any explanation he was about to give her ground to a halt. "We have to talk," he added after a very long pause.

"And you had to sneak in here and grab me to do that? You could have called."

"I had to see you in person, and I grabbed you because I didn't want you shouting out for someone. I didn't want to get shot before you listen to what I have to tell you. And you have to listen."

It was partly her bruised ego reacting, but

Addie huffed, folded her arms over her chest and glared at him. "You slept with me three months ago and then disappeared without so much as an email. Why should I listen to anything you have to say, huh?"

Still no quick answer. Probably because there wasn't one. Not one she'd want to hear anyway. But what she did want to hear was why he had on that gun holster that looked as if he'd been born to wear it. Also, why hadn't she been able to find out anything about him online?

Everything inside her went still.

"Who are you, *really*?" she asked.

Another long pause. "I'm not the man you think I am."

A burst of air left her mouth. Definitely not laughter. "Clearly. Now tell me something I don't know."

The hurt came hard and fast. Addie felt as if someone had put a vise around her heart. The tears quickly followed, too, and she tried hard to blink them away. No way did she want this man to see her cry.

"I'm sorry." He added more of that profanity and reached out as if he might pull her into his arms.

Addie put a stop to that. She batted his hands away. "You knew how vulnerable I was when you slept with me."

"Yes," he admitted. "You'd recently found out your birth father was a serial killer."

There it was, all wrapped up into one neat little summary. Stripped down to bare bones with no details. But the devil was in those details.

Well, one devil anyway.

Her biological father.

"Is everything you told me about your childhood the truth?" he asked.

She hadn't thought Wes could say anything that would surprise her, or stop her from forcing him to leave, but that did it. Addie just stared at him.

"When you were three, some ranch hands found you in the woods near here," Wes went on, obviously recapping details she already knew all too well. "You said you didn't remember your name, how you got there or anything about your past. You don't remember how you got *that*."

Before she could stop him, he brushed his fingers over her cheek. Over the small crescent-shaped scar that was there. It was faint now, just a thin whitish line next to her left eye, but Wes had obviously noticed it.

Addie flinched, backing away from him. What the heck was going on?

"Is all of that true?" he repeated.

Addie mustered up another huff and tried not to react to his touch. Wes didn't deserve a reaction. Too bad her body didn't understand that. Of course, her body was betraying her a lot lately.

"It's all true," she insisted.

For thirty years, Addie had tried not to think of herself as that wounded little girl in the woods with a cut on her face. Because she hadn't stayed there.

Thanks to Sheriff Sherman Crockett and his wife, Iris.

When no one had come forward to claim her after she'd been found, Sherman and Iris had adopted her, raised her along with their four sons on their Appaloosa Pass Ranch. They'd given her a name. A family. A wonderful life.

Until three months ago. Then, there'd been the DNA match that no one wanted. That's when her world was turned upside down.

"Why did your adoptive father put your DNA in the database when he found you?" Wes asked.

Again, it was another question she hadn't seen coming. Her adoptive father had been killed in the line of duty when she was just twelve, so she couldn't ask him directly, but Addie could guess why.

"Because he could have simply been looking to see if I matched anyone in the system. But I believe he wanted to find the birth parents who'd abandoned me and make them pay." That required a deep breath. "I'm positive he had no idea it'd lead to a killer."

And not just any old killer, either, but the Moonlight Strangler. He'd killed at least sixteen women, and fifteen of those crime scenes hadn't had a trace of his DNA. But three months ago number sixteen had. And while the DNA wasn't a match to any criminal already in the system, it had been a match to the killer's blood kin.

Addie.

Wes took her by the shoulders, forcing eye contact. "The Moonlight Strangler's really your father?"

It took Addie a moment to realize that it was actually a question. "Yes, according to the DNA match, he is. But Sherman Crockett was my father in the only way that will ever matter."

If only that were true.

Addie wanted it to be true. Desperately wanted it. But it was hard to push aside that she shared the blood and DNA of a serial killer.

"I need to hear it from you," Wes said. Not an order exactly. But it was close. "Is everything you said true? Do you have any memory whatsoever of why you were in those woods or who put you there?"

Addie threw up her hands. "Of course not. The FBI has questioned me over and over again.

They even had me hypnotized, and I remembered exactly what I'd already told everyone. Nothing."

She had no idea why Wes was asking these things, but it was time for Addie to turn the tables on him.

"Who are you?" she demanded. "And why are you here?"

His grip melted off her shoulders, and now it was Wes who moved away from her. "My real name is Weston Cade, and I'm a Texas Ranger."

Addie had to replay that several times before it sank in. After learning she was the daughter of a serial killer and having Wes leave without so much as a goodbye, she hadn't exactly had a rosy outlook on life. She'd braced herself in case Wes was about to confess that he, too, was some kind of criminal. But this revelation wasn't nearly as bad as the ones she had imagined.

"A Texas Ranger," she repeated. Addie shook her head. "You told me your name was Wes Martin and that you were a rodeo rider."

"Martin is my middle name, and I was a rodeo rider. Before I became a Ranger."

Her mouth tightened. "And I was a child before I became an adult. That doesn't make me a child now. You lied to me."

"Yeah." He nodded. "I didn't want you to know who I was and that I was investigating the Moonlight Strangler."

She stared at him, waiting for more. More that he didn't volunteer. "You were investigating him when you met me three months ago?"

No gaze-dodging this time. Wes, or rather *Weston*, looked her straight in the eyes. "I met you because I was looking for him. I followed you while you were in San Antonio, and after your interview with the FBI I followed you to the hotel where you were staying. I knew exactly who you were when I introduced myself at the bar."

That hit her like a heavyweight's punch, and Addie staggered back.

The memories of that first meeting were still so fresh in her mind. She'd been shaken to the core after the interview with the FBI, and even though her mother and one of her brothers had made the trip to San Antonio with her, she had asked for some alone time. And had ended up at the hotel bar.

Where she'd met Wes, a rodeo rider.

Or so she'd thought.

The attraction had been instant. Intense. Something Addie had never quite felt before. Of course, that intensity had dulled her instincts because she had believed with all her heart that this was a man who understood her. A man she could trust.

That was laughable now.

"Were you trying to get information from me?"

she asked, recalling all the words—the lies, no doubt—he'd told her that night.

A muscle flickered in his jaw.

Then Weston nodded.

She groaned, and now Addie was the one who cursed. "And you came back to the bar again the next night, after I'd been through the hypnosis. You knew I was an emotional wreck. You knew I was hanging by a thread, and yet you took me to your room and had sex with me. Not just that night, either, but the following night, too."

"That was never part of the plan," he said.

"The plan?" she snapped. "Well, your *plan* had consequences." Addie had another battle with tears, but thankfully she still managed to speak. "Leave now!"

Of course he didn't budge. Weston stayed put and took hold of her arm when she tried to bolt from the office.

The phone on her desk rang, the sound shooting through the room. Addie gasped before she realized that it wasn't the threat that her body was preparing itself for. The *threat* was in her office and had hold of her.

"Ignore that call. There are things you need to know," he insisted. "Things that might save your life."

That stopped Addie in her tracks, and she did indeed ignore the call. "What are you talking about?"

He didn't get a chance to answer because she heard another sound. Her mother's voice.

"Addie?" her mother called out. It sounded as if she was in the kitchen at the back of the house. "I picked up the phone when you didn't answer. It's about those mares you wanted to buy."

It was a call that Addie had been waiting on. An important one. Since she helped manage the ranch and the livestock, it was her job. But she was afraid her job would have to wait.

"Tell her to take a message," Weston instructed.

Addie wanted to tell him a flat-out no. She didn't want to obey orders from this lying Texas Ranger who'd taken her to his bed with the notion of getting information she didn't even have.

"Why should I?" she snarled.

"Because you're in danger. Your mother could be, too."

Addie had been certain that there was nothing Weston could say that would make her agree to his order.

Nothing except that.

"Mom," Addie said after a serious debate with herself. "Take a message. I'll return the call soon."

She hoped.

"Start talking," Addie told Weston. "Tell me exactly what's going on."

But he didn't say anything. Instead, he started to unbutton his shirt.

Either he'd lost his mind, or…

It was *or.*

Addie saw the scar on his chest. The long jagged cut that wasn't nearly as faded and healed as the one on her face. It was one that she'd already noticed the night they'd landed in bed together. Weston had told her he'd been hooked by a bull's horn at a rodeo.

"The Moonlight Strangler did this to me," Weston said. "Your *father* nearly killed me."

Oh, God.

"You know who my birth father is?" She couldn't ask that fast enough.

"No. I didn't see his face. And I didn't have any leads to his identity until I found out the results of your DNA test."

Addie's heart was pounding now. Her breath thin. "You thought he'd come to me?"

Weston nodded. "I counted on it. I know your DNA match was supposed to be kept quiet, but I figured if I could find out about it, then so could the killer."

It took her a moment to gather her voice. "You leaked my DNA results?" She shoved Weston away from her and would have bolted, but, like before, he held on.

"No," he insisted. "But someone might have. Maybe a dirty cop or someone in the crime lab who was paid off."

"Or it could have been you. And to think, I slept with you, not just that one night, either, but the following night, too. I..." Addie stopped because there was no way she would give him another emotional piece of herself. "You used me as bait."

Her voice hardly had sound now, but that didn't mean she wasn't feeling every inch of the proverbial knife he'd stuck in her back.

"No," Weston repeated. "But someone did. And it worked."

There went the rest of her breath. "Who? How?"

Weston shook his head. "I don't know the who or the how, but I know the results." He looked her straight in the eyes. "Addie, you're the Moonlight Strangler's next target."

# *Chapter Two*

Weston waited for Addie's reaction, and he didn't have to wait long.

She shook her head, her bottom lip trembling just a little before she clamped her teeth over it. It only took a few seconds for Addie to process what Weston had just told her.

And to dismiss it.

"Why should I believe anything you say?" she asked.

Weston had no trouble hearing the hurt in her voice. No trouble hearing the anger, too. Yes, he was responsible for both, and while he'd never intended to hurt Addie, he also hadn't wanted a serial killer to have free rein to keep on killing. Too bad he'd failed.

Addie was indeed hurt.

And the killer was still out there.

Of course, Addie knew that better than anyone else: her own sister-in-law had been one of the Moonlight Strangler's victims.

"I'm sorry," Weston said, knowing his words wouldn't be worth much. "But it's true. I have proof the Midnight Strangler's coming after you, and we need to talk about that."

Judging from the way her eyes narrowed, he'd been right about that apology not meaning much.

Addie didn't jump to ask about his *proof*.

Her blond hair was gathered into a ponytail, but she swiped away the strands that'd fallen onto her face during their scuffle, and she whirled around so that she was no longer facing him. At least she didn't try to make a run out of her office again, but she might do just that before this conversation was over.

Even though it had only been three months since Weston had seen her, she'd changed plenty. He had watched her for about a half hour before he'd gotten the chance to pull her into the office for a private chat. When she was in the barn earlier, Addie had been working with one of the horses, and she had actually smiled a time or two. She looked content. Happy, even.

Definitely something he hadn't seen when she was in San Antonio.

There, she'd been wearing dresses more suited for office work than the jeans and denim shirt she was wearing now. And she definitely hadn't been happy or smiling during their chats at the bar and in his hotel room.

No.

Most of the time, she'd been on the verge of losing it, and had been trying to come to terms with learning exactly who she was. Weston certainly hadn't helped with the situation by sleeping with her.

After several long moments, she turned back around to face him. In the same motion, she took out her phone from her jeans pocket. "I'm calling Jericho."

Jericho, her oldest adopted brother. He was also the sheriff in the nearby town of Appaloosa Pass, the job once held by her late father. Weston definitely didn't want to tangle with any of the Crockett lawmen, not just yet anyway, so that's why he reached for her phone.

"I want to find out who you really are," Addie snapped. "And you're *not* going to stop me from doing that."

It was a risk in case she tried to get her brother to arrest him or something, but Weston decided to see how this played out. Eventually, he'd have to deal with Jericho anyway. It was a meeting he wasn't exactly looking forward to since Jericho had a reputation for being a badass, no-shades-of-gray kind of lawman.

"Jericho," Addie said when her brother answered. She put the call on speaker. "I need a favor. Can you check and see if there's a Texas Ranger by the name of Weston Cade?"

Weston heard Jericho's brief silence. Was he suspicious? Definitely. But the question was—what would Jericho do about it? If he came storming back to the house, it might trigger something Weston didn't want triggered.

"Why?" her brother asked her.

"Just do it," Addie insisted, "*please*." She sounded more like an annoyed sister than a woman whose lip had been trembling just moments earlier.

More silence from Jericho, followed by some mumblings, but Weston did hear the clicks of a computer keyboard.

"Yeah, he's a Ranger in the San Antonio unit," her brother verified. "Why?" Jericho repeated, but he didn't wait for an answer. "And does he have anything to do with that SOB scumbag you met in San Antonio, the one who slept with you and—"

"I'll call you back," Addie interrupted, and she hung up. She dodged his gaze when she slid her phone back into her pocket.

Weston doubted she'd put a quick end to that call for his sake, but it did give him a glimpse of what she'd been going through for three months. She had obviously told Jericho about her brief affair with a man who'd seemingly disappeared from the face of the earth, and her brother clearly didn't have a high opinion of him.

*SOB scumbag.*

Well, the label fit. Weston didn't have a high opinion of himself, either, and he hadn't in a very long time.

Addie wouldn't believe that he had plenty of regrets when it came to her. After all his lies, she would never believe that he'd fallen in bed with her only because of the intense attraction he had felt for her.

An attraction he still felt.

Still, he shouldn't have acted on it. He should have just kept his distance and tailed her until her father made his move, no matter how long that took.

"Start from the beginning," Addie insisted, turning her attention back to Weston. "And so help me, every word coming out of your mouth had better be the truth, or I'll let Jericho have a go at you. I don't make a habit of letting my big brother fight my battles for me, but in your case I'll make an exception."

Weston figured that wasn't a bluff.

The *beginning* required him to take a deep breath. "Two years ago I went to my fiancée's office to see her. I'd just come off an undercover assignment and hadn't seen her in a few weeks.

Her name was Collette, and I walked in on someone murdering her."

Hell, it hurt to say that aloud. It didn't set well with Addie, either, because she made a slight gasping sound.

"It was my birth father," she supplied. "I saw a list of his known victims. All sixteen of them, and Collette Metcalf was one of them."

Weston nodded, and it took him a moment to trust his voice again. "I didn't know it was him at the time, and I didn't get a look at his face because he knifed me and ran out. I obviously survived, but Collette wasn't so lucky. She died by the time the ambulance arrived."

She touched her fingers to her mouth. It was trembling again, and Addie leaned against the edge of her desk, no doubt for support. "Your name wasn't in the reports I read of the murders."

"No. The FBI and Rangers thought it best if they didn't make it public. They didn't want him coming after me to tie up loose ends. The killer hadn't gotten a good look at my face because I was still wearing my undercover disguise. But he must have found out who I was because letters from the Moonlight Strangler started arriving three months ago."

"Three months?" she repeated under her breath.

Addie no doubt picked up on the timing.

Weston doubted it was a coincidence that the letters started arriving shortly after he met her.

"The killer mentions me in these letters?" she asked, and Weston had to nod.

That meant the Moonlight Strangler had perhaps already been watching Addie and had seen Weston with her. Or maybe the killer had been watching him. Either way, Weston figured the killer had started sending those letters because he knew about Addie and him sleeping together.

"All the letters and envelopes were typed," Weston continued, "so there's no handwriting to be analyzed. No fibers or trace on any of them. They were mailed from various locations all over the state."

Addie shook her head. "How can you be sure they're from the killer?"

"Because there are details in them that were withheld from the press. Details that only the Moonlight Strangler would know."

She stayed quiet a moment. "The letters threatened you?"

"Taunted me," Weston corrected. With details of Collette's murder...and other things. I tried to draw the killer out. I made sure my address was public. I put out the word through criminal informants that I wanted to meet with him, but he wouldn't come after me."

"You made yourself bait," Addie corrected.

"Plenty of times."

Weston had failed at that, too.

"The killer's never contacted me," she said. "Of course I've been worried…scared," Addie corrected, "that he would. Or that he would do even more than just contact me." She paused. "How did you find out I was his biological daughter?"

"I was keeping tabs on anything to do with the Moonlight Strangler. As a Texas Ranger, I have access to the DNA databases, and I'd hoped there'd be a DNA match to someone."

Her next breath was mixed with a sigh. "And there was. Then, because you'd found out I was his biological daughter, you…what?" No more sighing. Her eyes narrowed. "You thought he'd want to connect with the child he abandoned in the woods nearly thirty years ago?"

Her anger was back. Good. It was actually easier for him to deal with than the fear and hurt. But unfortunately, he was going to have to tell her something that would bring the fear back with a vengeance.

"Yesterday, I got this." Weston took the paper from his pocket and turned on the light so she could better see it. "It's the eighth letter he's sent me. It's a copy, not the original, so it's okay for you to handle it."

She didn't take it at first. Addie just volleyed glances between him and the paper before she finally eased it out of his hand, taking it only by the corner as if she didn't want to touch too much of it.

Since Weston knew every word that was written there, he watched Addie's reaction. The shock.

And yes, the fear.

"'Tell Addie that it's time for me to end what I started thirty years ago,'" she read aloud. She paused. "'I can't have a little girl's memories coming back to haunt me.'"

Her gaze skirted over the words again. She cleared her throat before her gaze came back to his.

"This is why you asked if I remembered anything," Addie said. "I don't," she quickly added.

"And you don't remember that?" He tipped his head to the scar on her cheek.

"No." She handed him back the letter. "Did he cut the other women he killed like this?"

Weston settled for a nod. "That was kept out of the reports to the press, too. Only a handful of people know that he cut them first. Then strangled them."

"I see." Her mouth tightened a moment. "I'd always hoped I got the scar from a tree branch or something."

Yes, since that was far better than the alternative. Because that scar on her face meant the

Moonlight Strangler had already gone after her once. When she was just three years old.

Now he was coming for her again.

"The killer could be worried that you remembered something in that hypnosis session," Weston said. "Or that you might remember something in the future. The FBI wants to do more sessions with you, right?"

She nodded, confirming what he already knew. Nearly every law enforcement agency in the state as well as the FBI wanted to keep pressing her to remember.

"We don't have much time," Weston continued. "He usually strikes on the night of a full or half moon. Like tonight."

Her attention drifted to the window where she could see that the sun was only minutes away from setting. Something else flashed through her eyes. Not fear this time. But major concern.

"My mother's in the house. And the ranch hands—"

Weston stepped in front of her to keep her from leaving. "They're okay. For now. It's you he wants, and, other than me, he hasn't attacked or hurt anyone else when he murdered his victims."

Of course, since Addie was his daughter, the killer might make a really big exception. That was what Weston had to guard against.

She frantically shook her head. “Has he ever named victims before he killed them?”

“Never.”

“Then you have no way of knowing that he won’t go after my mother. Heck, my entire family.” A clipped sob tore from her throat. “I can’t let him get to them.”

“I’ve already arranged for someone to watch the road leading to the ranch. I won’t let him hurt them.” Weston hoped that was a promise he could keep. He didn’t have a good track record when it came to stopping this vicious killer.

“Who?” she pressed.

“Friends I can trust. I didn’t want to involve the Rangers in this because I’m trying to set a trap for the killer, and I didn’t want him hearing about it. But these friends are armed, and they’ll let me know if he tries to get to you.”

That was part of the plan anyway.

But not all of it.

“I don’t just want to scare off the Moonlight Strangler,” Weston explained. “I want to catch him. *Tonight*.”

Addie froze. Then her breath shivered. “You want to use me to draw him out.”

“Yes.” Hard for Weston to admit that, but it was the truth. “We know he’ll probably come here, and since he doesn’t know that I’ve contacted you—”

“What if the letter is a hoax?” she interrupted.

"I mean, why tell you what he's going to do? He must know that as a Texas Ranger you'd try to warn me."

"That's not the only reason I would have warned you." Judging from the hard look she gave him, she didn't believe it.

He took out the copy of the second letter. "It came the same time as the other one, but it was a different envelope." Weston unfolded it, held it up for Addie to see. "If you try to save Addie, I'll kill Isabel and you," he read.

"Isabel?" she asked.

"My kid sister. She's in medical school. I've already had her put in protective custody. Now the next step is doing the same for you, but that's why I snuck onto the ranch. I didn't want the killer to know I'd come here. It might have provoked him or sent him into a rage."

Not that a serial killer didn't already have enough rage. Still, Weston had wanted to try to control the situation as much as he could.

The silence came. Addie, staring at him. Obviously trying to make sense of this. He wanted to tell her there was nothing about this that made sense because they were dealing with a very dangerous, very crazy man.

"Oh, God," she finally said.

Now her fear was sky-high, and Weston held his breath. He didn't expect Addie to go blindly along with a plan to stop her father. But she did want to stop the Moonlight Strangler from claiming another victim.

Weston was counting heavily on that.

However, Addie shook her head. "I can't help you."

That sure wasn't the reaction Weston had expected. He'd figured Addie was as desperate to end this as he was.

She squeezed her eyes shut a moment. "I'll get my mother, and we can go to the sheriff's office. Two of my brothers are there, and they can make sure this monster stays far away from us."

"You'll be safe at the sheriff's office," Weston agreed, "but you can't stay there forever. Neither can your family. Eventually, you'll have to leave, and the killer will come after you."

"That can't happen!" Addie groaned and looked up at the ceiling as if she expected some kind of divine help. "I can't be in that kind of danger."

Weston tried to keep his voice as calm as possible. Hard to do, though, with the emotions swirling like a tornado inside him. "I'm sorry. If there was another way to stop him, then I wouldn't have come here. I know I don't have a right to ask, but I need your help."

"I can't."

"You can't? Convince me why," Weston snapped. "Because I'm not getting this. You must want this killer off the street. It's the only way you'll ever be truly safe."

Addie opened her mouth. Closed it. And she stared at him. "I'd planned on telling you. Not like this. But if I ever saw you again, I intended to tell you."

There was a new emotion in her voice and on her face. One that Weston couldn't quite put his finger on. "Tell me what?" he asked.

She dragged in a long breath and straightened her shoulders. "I can't be bait for the Moonlight Strangler because I can't risk being hurt." Addie took another deep breath. "I'm three months pregnant. And the baby is *yours*."

# Chapter Three

Addie figured this was the worst way possible a man could find out that he'd fathered a child.

But she hadn't exactly had a choice about the timing of the news. Weston had come here to drop a bombshell that he wanted to use her to catch a killer, that the killer was actually after her, but she'd delivered her own bombshell.

And it had stunned him to silence.

Weston just stared at her for a very long time, and she could almost see the wheels turning in his head. This pregnancy changed everything.

At least it had for Addie.

Maybe it would for Weston, too.

Change him in a way that wouldn't put her in danger. Three months ago, she would have been willing to do whatever it took to catch the Moonlight Strangler. Weston obviously felt the same way. Especially since the killer had murdered a woman he loved. But even though the killer had murdered her brother's wife, Addie couldn't allow herself to be used in this justice net.

Unless…

"Can you guarantee me that the baby wouldn't be hurt?" However, she waved off the question as soon as she asked it. "You and I both know you can't. The Moonlight Strangler's smart. He's been killing and evading the law for three decades, maybe more, and he might have already figured out a way to get around you so he could come after me."

Heck, the killer might have figured out a way to use Weston. Too bad Addie couldn't think of how he'd done that, and she didn't want to find out the hard way, either. This had to end.

But how?

"You're pregnant," Weston said under his breath. He groaned, and this time he was the one to do the stepping away.

She couldn't blame him for being stunned. The truth was, Addie had been pretty darn stunned herself when she'd first learned the news. She had always wanted children and figured that one day she would be a mom. She just hadn't thought it would happen like this, with her being unmarried and with the baby's father disappearing.

Weston shook his head. "But we used protection."

Ironic that she had said the exact same thing

to the doctor when he'd confirmed the pregnancy test results. That day, she'd said a lot of things, including some profanity in regards to Weston.

"Obviously, protection's not a hundred percent. Don't worry," Addie quickly added. "I was going to tell you if I ever managed to locate you, but I don't need anything from you, including child support. Or any other kind of support for that matter. As far as I'm concerned, you won't be a part of this."

The look he gave her could have blasted a giant hole through the moon. Weston's eyes went to slits, and the muscles in his face turned to iron. "It's my baby. I'll be a part of *this*."

"That's not necessary—"

"I'll be part of his or her life," he insisted.

All right. She hadn't exactly counted on that reaction. "After you ran out on me, I figured..."

Considering that his eyes narrowed even more, it was probably best not to finish spelling out that she didn't believe him to be the sort who stuck around. Even for his own child.

And then it hit her.

Addie really didn't know him. Didn't know anything real about his life because of all the lies he'd told her.

"Are you married?" she asked.

That didn't do much to help with those narrowed eyes. "No. I wouldn't have slept with you if I'd been married."

She let that hum between them, but hopefully he understood what she was thinking. A man who'd lie and then have sex with a troubled woman didn't exactly have a stellar moral compass.

"And no, I'm not involved with anyone," he went on. "Not now, and not when I was with you."

"Why did you sleep with me?" she demanded.

Mercy, she wanted to kick herself for blurting that out. Not because she didn't want to know the truth.

She did.

But Addie was a thousand percent certain that she wasn't up to hearing it spelled out now. Not with all the other news that Weston had just delivered.

Now he looked at her, and that wasn't a glare in his smoky brown eyes.

Nope.

It was a look he'd given her many times over the three days when they'd been together. It was something she felt right after she first met him.

Something she didn't want to feel, but Addie felt it again anyway.

The heat came like a touch. Barely a brush against her skin. But it rippled through her. Gently. At first. Until the ripple became a tug and made her recall exactly why she'd landed in bed with Weston.

"Yeah," he said. "Remember now?"

Since a lie would stick in her throat, Addie settled for a nod. "But I slept with you only because of the attraction. Can you say the same?"

No quick answer. Not verbally anyway, but she got another glare from him. She'd always thought Jericho was the king of glares and surly expressions, but right now Weston had her brother beat by a mile.

"Like I said, that wasn't part of the plan," Weston finally repeated. "It just...happened."

She had the feeling he'd intended to say something else, but it was best if this part of the conversation ended. Addie didn't need any other reminders of the heat that'd been between them then.

And now.

"Sleeping with me wasn't part of this grand plan you keep mentioning," she said, trying to get her thoughts back on track. "But leaving was."

"I left because of the letters," Weston clarified, though she didn't know how he managed to speak through clenched teeth. "The killer warned me to stay away from you."

Addie hadn't thought there'd be any more surprises today, but she'd been wrong. Her heartbeat kicked up again, drumming in her ears. "Why did he give you a warning like that?"

"He didn't want us teaming up to find him," Weston readily answered. "He said he'd kill you if I stayed. That you'd live if I left."

That sent another rush of emotions through her. For three months, Addie had dealt with the anger and hurt of having Weston walk out. In the past fifteen minutes, she'd had to deal with the news that her biological father was coming after her.

Now this.

If Weston had indeed left to try to save her, then that put him in a new light. One she wasn't ready to deal with just yet. After all, he had known who she was when he'd slept with her, and she wasn't ready to forgive him for that just yet.

Maybe not ever.

As raw as her emotions were and despite the fact Weston was still glaring at her, Addie had to push all that aside. Yes, she'd have to deal with it later, but for now they had a more immediate problem on their hands, and protecting the baby and her family had to come first. That meant making sure she was protected, as well.

Addie didn't intend to rely on Weston for that.

"I need to tell Jericho about the threatening letters you got," she said, thinking out loud.

However, she didn't even get a chance to reach for her phone before she heard the footsteps behind her in the hall. Weston obviously heard them, too, because he moved fast. A lot faster than Addie. He latched on to her arm, dragging her behind him, and in the same motion, he drew his gun.

Just like that, Addie's heart jumped to her throat, and the danger to her unborn child and family came at her like an avalanche. However, the threat that her body was preparing her for turned out not to be a threat after all.

"Put down that gun, and let go of my daughter," her mother demanded. She had something to back up that demand, too. Her mother aimed a double-barreled shotgun at Weston.

The relief hit Addie almost as hard as the slam of fear had, so it took her a moment to speak. It wasn't the killer, but her mother was limping her way toward them. "It's okay, Mom."

That wasn't exactly the truth. Everything was far from being okay, but Addie didn't want her mother pointing a gun at a Texas Ranger.

Even *this* Ranger.

Her mother obviously didn't buy her *it's okay* because she didn't lower the gun, and she continued to volley glances between Weston and Addie. Even though she wasn't a large woman, and her hair was completely silver-gray, she still managed to look tough as nails.

"Who is he?" her mother asked. But almost immediately her gaze dropped to Addie's stomach.

"Yes, he's the baby's father," Addie verified. "Mom, this is Weston Cade. Weston, this is my mom, Iris Crockett."

It seemed silly to make polite introductions at a time like this, but it did get her mother to lower the shotgun. What her mom didn't do was ease up on the glare she was giving Weston.

"You hurt my daughter," her mother said.

"I know," Weston readily admitted. "And I'm sorry." He, too, put away his gun, sliding it back into his holster.

Her mother didn't say the words, but her frosty blue eyes let Weston know that his apology alone wouldn't be nearly good enough. Maybe nothing would be. After all, her mother had no doubt heard Addie's crying jags and had seen the hurt and sadness.

"How did you get inside?" her mother asked Weston. "I didn't hear you ring the doorbell, and if you had, I wouldn't have let you in."

"He came in with me from the barn," Addie jumped to answer. Best if her mother didn't know she'd just been in a partial wrestling match with the man who'd fathered her child. "Weston has bad news. Well, maybe it's bad. If the letters he got are real, then it's bad."

"They're real," Weston insisted.

Again, her mother didn't say anything, but she grasped it right away. "This is about the Moonlight Strangler." Still limping, she moved protectively to Addie's side, slipping her left arm around her. "Is he coming after Addie?"

That was something both she and her mother had no doubt asked themselves dozens of times, but they'd never spoken of it.

Too frightening to consider aloud.

Of course, Addie had taken precautions. Always looking over her shoulder. Always on guard for her biological father to make some kind of contact. Or try to murder her. But after three months of the precautions, Addie had thought she was safe.

"I need to talk to Jericho," Addie said, taking out her phone. "I'll have him come home right away. Jax, too."

She almost explained to Weston that Jax was a deputy in Appaloosa Pass, but there was probably little about her and her family that he didn't already know. Well, with the exception of the pregnancy, but then there were only six people who'd known about that: her mother, her four brothers and the doctor.

"I'll alert the ranch hands so they can all get inside the bunkhouse," her mother added.

But Weston took hold of both their arms before either of them could make those calls. "If the

Moonlight Strangler suspects you're on to him, he won't come here."

Her mother gave a crisp nod. "Good!"

"Not good." Addie groaned. "Because he might try to go after Weston's sister. Or he'll just wait to attack again."

Weston was right. They couldn't live at the sheriff's office or stay locked up in the house. They had a huge ranch to run. Plus, there was the baby. Addie didn't want her child to be a prisoner because they had had the bad luck to wind up in the wrong gene pool.

"So, what do we do?" Addie asked, hating that she didn't already have a plan. One that didn't involve Weston and that could ensure her baby wouldn't be hurt.

Weston opened his mouth to answer, but before he could say a word, Addie's phone rang. It wasn't Jericho's name she saw on the screen, however. It was Teddy McQueen, one of the ranch hands.

"If this is about those mares," Addie said the moment she answered, "we'll have to discuss it another time."

"Addie," the man said. His voice was barely a whisper.

"What's wrong?" she asked.

For several snail-crawling moments, all she heard was Teddy's ragged breath. That didn't help steady her nerves. Weston's either, because he took the phone from her and jabbed the speaker button.

"I was in the south pasture and spotted someone by the shed there," Teddy finally continued. "A man. I was about to ask him what he was doing, and he shot me with one of those guns fitted with a silencer. I didn't even see it until it was too late."

"Oh, God. Call nine-one-one and get an ambulance," Addie told her mother, and Iris immediately did that. "Teddy, how bad are you hurt?"

"Not sure. But the bullet's in my leg so I can't walk."

"Just hold on. We'll get someone out to you," Addie assured him.

"Tell whoever's coming to be careful. *Real* careful. You and Iris, too. I didn't get a look at the man's face, but I saw what direction he went."

Teddy took another long breath. "Addie, you need to watch out. He's headed straight for the house."

# *Chapter Four*

Weston's first instinct was to curse. And to punch himself for not fixing this before the danger was right on Addie's doorstep.

Why the heck hadn't his *friends* warned him?

Later, he'd want an answer to that, but he had to focus on making sure this situation didn't go from bad to worse. For now, Weston settled for firing off a quick text to one of those friends to warn him that all hell had broken loose.

"How long do we have before the man gets here?" Addie asked the wounded ranch hand.

"He's on foot, but he's moving pretty quick. You got fifteen minutes, maybe less."

Weston figured with the way his luck had been running, it'd be *less*. That wasn't enough time for Jericho to make it out to the ranch, but maybe it was enough for Weston's friends to get onto the grounds and help.

The moment he finished the text, Weston slapped off the lights, pulled Addie's mom into the office with them and then closed the blinds. "Get down on the floor behind the desk. I'll go through the house and lock the doors."

"It'll go faster if I show you where all the doors are," Addie insisted.

"Or I could go," Iris volunteered.

Addie shook her head. "Not with your sore ankle. I can move a lot faster than you can. You wait here and keep watch while I go with Weston."

Normally, he would have refused her help, but it was a big place even by Texas standards, and he didn't want to miss an entrance.

"All right." Iris shifted her shotgun so that it'd be easier for her to use. "I'll call Jericho. Just hurry and get back here."

Weston nodded. "Tell the other ranch hands, too, so they'll get inside and take cover. I also want you to stay away from the windows."

He wasn't sure the Moonlight Strangler was into shooting bystanders, but Weston didn't want to take any chances. Not with Iris. Not with Addie. Especially since she was pregnant with his child.

Later, he'd need to settle that with Addie.

And himself.

Weston figured he'd be asking himself a lot of "what the hell have I done?" questions.

"This way," Addie said, leading him not to the front of the house but rather the back.

She was focused on the task. Or rather trying

to pretend she was. But Weston could still feel the fear coming from her. Could also feel her dodging his gaze. He couldn't blame her. She probably didn't want to trust him, but at the moment she had no choice.

"Your friends didn't see the killer when he shot Teddy," she said like the accusation that it was.

"Apparently not," he settled for saying.

"And you still trust them?" Again, an accusation.

"Yeah. With my life."

She glanced at him, a reminder that he'd trusted them with her life, too. And her mother's. The glance was well deserved. He had done just that. But both of his friends were former cops and had plenty of equipment that should have detected anyone in those woods surrounding the ranch.

It was obviously a precaution that'd failed bigtime.

Addie and he threaded their way through a massive family room, turning off lights and locking two doors there before doing the same to yet three more off the kitchen and adjoining dining room. Even though Christmas was still three weeks away, everything was decorated for the holiday. Trees, wreaths and other decorations were in almost every room.

"My mother goes a little overboard. She loves Christmas," Addie said.

Maybe because Addie had been found nearly thirty years ago on Christmas Eve. From everything Weston had uncovered, Iris had always wanted a daughter, so this could be a dual celebration of sorts.

Next, there was another office. Jericho's no doubt, judging from the man-cave decor. And across the hall was a playroom filled with toys and books—a reminder that Addie had a nephew. Thank Heaven the little boy wasn't in the house, because it was more than enough just protecting Addie and her mother.

"The windows upstairs have child locks on them and are wired in case my nephew tries to open them," Addie explained. The words practically ran together, even faster than she was jetting around the house.

He doubted the Moonlight Strangler would climb a ladder to try to get inside. That would make him too visible, but he might try other ways. "Is there a security system for the rest of the house?"

Addie nodded, her breath still gusting. "Jericho had one installed after...well, just after."

It was the kind of security measure Weston would have taken if he'd been in her brother's place, even if there'd been no hint of the killer coming after her.

"It's not armed," he reminded her. Weston knew

that for a fact since he'd literally walked right into the house. Something he needed to stop the killer from doing.

"The keypad is by the front door." Addie led him in that direction, and while she set the system, Weston locked that door. He also checked the sidelight windows.

No one was out there. Yet. If a killer hadn't had a target on Addie, everything would have seemed normal. Well, everything outside anyway.

"Does the alarm cover all the windows and doors?" Weston asked.

She nodded. "But it won't go off if the glass breaks. Only if a window is actually lifted."

That was better than nothing.

Weston took Addie back to her office. Not ideal since there was a big window, but all the rooms on the bottom floor had them.

"Jericho's on the way," Iris informed them the moment they returned. "An ambulance, too. I called Teddy again and told him to hold on."

Maybe holding on would be enough and an ambulance could get to the ranch hand before he bled out. Of course, Jericho likely wouldn't let the ambulance onto the grounds unless he was certain it was safe for the medics.

And with a killer out there, it was far from safe.

"Get down," Weston reminded Addie when she

hurried to a cabinet in the corner, where she took down a gun off the top shelf.

Good. He hated that she had to be armed, hated she was terrified to the point of shaking, but without backup, Weston wanted all the help he could get.

With his gun ready, he hurried to the window, staying to the side but still putting himself in a position so he could look out and keep watch. Weston lifted one of the blind slats, bracing himself for the worst. His heart nearly jumped from his chest when the lights flared on.

He cursed.

And it took him a second to realize it wasn't the glare of something from the killer. It was Christmas lights. Hundreds of them. They were strung out across the barns, shrubs, porch and fences, and they winked on and off, the little blasts of color slicing through the darkness.

"They're on a timer," Addie said. That's when he realized she had lifted her head and was looking out, as well. He motioned for her to get back down. "You want me to turn them off?"

"No."

They actually helped by lighting up the grounds, and it would make it harder for the killer to use the darkness to hide. Weston hoped. This wasn't the Moonlight Strangler's first rodeo, and he'd likely already cased the ranch to find the safest path for him to launch an attack.

Too bad there were plenty of places to do just that.

"Why is this monster doing this now, after all this time?" Iris asked.

While Addie filled her in on what they knew, Weston kept watch and took out his phone to call Cliff Romero, a former cop and one of the friends he'd positioned around the grounds surrounding the Crockett ranch.

"What went wrong?" Weston asked the moment Cliff answered.

"We're not sure. He didn't get past Dave and me."

Dave Roper. The other former cop out there. Both men had been armed with thermal equipment that should have detected anyone or anything with a pulse.

And that could mean only one thing.

That the killer had already been on the ranch grounds, maybe waiting in the shed for nightfall. He was also likely wearing some kind of clothing that would make it hard for the equipment to detect him.

"Hell," Weston said under his breath.

"My thoughts exactly. Dave and I are moving closer, hoping to pick up his trail. Make sure we're not hit with friendly fire."

"I'll try." He hung up and glanced back at Addie again. "Text Jericho and let him know there are two PIs headed in the direction of the house."

She did. But that didn't mean Dave and Cliff were safe. He only hoped the pair caught up with the killer before he could inflict more harm.

"Maybe he'll just leave if he knows we're onto him," Iris whispered.

Yeah, he probably would, and it was tempting to shout out something or fire a warning shot. But if Weston did that, it wouldn't end the threat. It would only postpone an attack to another place, another time. One when Weston might have a lesser chance of protecting Addie.

"Do you see him?" Addie asked.

Weston shook his head and tried to think of something reassuring to say. He failed. Addie no doubt saw the worry on his face and in his body language. And he was indeed worried. Even if the killer didn't attack, all of this stress couldn't be good for Addie and the baby.

The moments crawled by. Turning into minutes. Still no sign of the Moonlight Strangler. No sign of his friends or Jericho, either.

But Weston sensed something.

Exactly what, he wasn't sure, but he felt the knot tighten in his gut. Felt that warning slide down his spine. A warning that'd saved his butt a time or two. And that's why he ducked back from the window.

Not a second too soon.

The bullet crashed through the glass in the exact spot where Weston had just been standing.

He'd braced himself for an attack, of course, but Weston doubted anyone could brace themselves for the roaring blast from the shot and the instant surge of adrenaline through their body.

"Stay down!" he warned Addie and her mother. He hoped the ranch hands were doing the same thing.

A second shot came. Then another.

Both went through what was left of the window and slammed into the wall behind him. They also helped him pinpoint the location of the shooter. All three shots had come from the area around the barn nearest the house.

The killer was way too close.

Not as close as he'd been when he had murdered Collette and left Weston for dead, but it was the first time Weston had been in a position to get a glimpse of him since that fateful night.

The rage roared through him. Not a good mix with the adrenaline and other things he was feeling, but Weston refused to let this snake go after anyone else. Especially Addie.

"Are there any ranch hands in the barn out there?" Weston tipped his head in that direction.

"There shouldn't be," Addie answered.

Good. That'd be fewer targets for this idiot to try to kill. And the man was definitely trying to kill them. Weston had no doubts about that as even more bullets crashed through the window.

It was always unnerving to have shots fired, but it didn't help that knot in his stomach when the killer stopped shooting.

Did that mean he was on the move?

Probably. Because it was too much to hope that he'd run out of ammunition.

Weston ducked and hurried to the other side of the window. It was a better vantage point if the shooter was headed to the back of the house, but Weston still didn't see anything.

Not at first anyway.

Finally, the Christmas lights flickered over a shadowy spot by one of the trucks parked between the house and the barn. Yeah, someone was definitely there.

Weston took aim and fired.

And he got confirmation of the guy's location when he saw him scramble behind the truck. He also got another confirmation he'd been waiting for—the sound of sirens from a police cruiser. Jericho, no doubt.

But Weston obviously wasn't the only one who knew that backup was about to arrive. He saw the shooter dart out from the back of the truck. And the man took off running.

Hell.

Weston didn't want this monster to get away, and that's exactly what would happen if he waited for Jericho. It'd be a minute or more before Addie's brother could stop the cruiser and get into place.

A minute the killer would use to escape.

It was a risk. A huge one. Anything Weston did at this point would be.

He fired a glance at Addie. "Text Jericho and tell him where you are. Then stay down and shoot anyone who tries to come in through this window." He also tossed her his phone. "Text the first contact in there and let him know I'm out of the house."

She was shaking her head before he even finished. "You can't go out there," Addie insisted.

"I can't let him get away," he insisted right back. He knocked out the rest of the shards of glass from the window.

Weston wished he had the time to convince her that this was the only way, but he didn't. With Jericho so close now, he'd be able to protect Addie and their mother. But just in case the killer doubled back and tried to come through the window, Weston kept watch around him.

And he started running the moment his feet hit the ground.

For one thing, he wanted to get out of the line of fire in case Jericho mistook him for the killer. For another, he wanted to make up the distance between him and the guy he could see running flat-out ahead of him.

Weston could also see something else thanks to the Christmas lights.

The guy was dressed all in black and was wearing a ski mask, and he wasn't running in a straight line. He was darting in and out of whatever he could use for cover. In addition to a gun, he was also carrying something else.

Something that he tossed onto the ground after glancing back over his shoulder at Weston.

Weston darted around whatever he'd tossed, hoping like the devil that it wasn't a bomb or explosive device, but it wasn't.

It appeared to be a thermal scanner like the one Dave and Cliff had been using.

That was probably why the killer had managed to pinpoint them so quickly in the house. After all, he hadn't fired any shots except right into the office, where they'd been hiding.

Behind him, Weston could hear the cruiser approaching, and the slashing blue lights blended with those from the Christmas decorations. It didn't create the best setup for spotting a killer since it was playing havoc with his vision. But Weston kept on running. Kept looking over his shoulder to make sure this snake didn't have a partner who was trying to go after Addie.

The killer scurried out of cover, headed toward a second barn. Weston wasn't sure if there were vehicles inside or not, but he didn't want to chance it.

Weston stopped. And he took aim.

He didn't aim for the guy's head. Something he desperately wanted to do. Especially with all the rage he was feeling. He could avenge Collette's death right here, right now. No judge, no jury.

Just one executioner with really good aim.

However, if Weston did that, he wouldn't get answers, and there were a lot of families out there looking for missing loved ones that this piece of dirt could have murdered. Besides, Weston wanted to look this killer in the eyes and make him answer for what he'd done.

Weston fired.

The shot went exactly where he'd intended it to go. In the killer's right shoulder. It worked because the guy tumbled onto the ground.

"Move and the next bullets go in your kneecaps," Weston warned him.

Weston wasted no time going after him, and it wasn't long before he got close enough to see the killer's face. Or rather the ski mask he was wearing. He was bleeding, clutching his shoulder with his left hand.

But not his right.

Despite the injury, he was reaching for his gun that had fallen just inches away from him.

"You really want to die tonight?" Weston warned him, and he aimed his gun right at the killer's head.

The killer did move, though, but only to lift both his hands. Weston hurried to kick the gun aside so that the guy couldn't change his mind and reach for it.

Then, Weston did some reaching of his own.

He had to see the killer's face. Had to stare down the man who'd murdered Collette. He ripped off the ski mask, and he got a good look at him all right.

Weston cursed.

*No.*

# *Chapter Five*

Addie wasn't sure who was more frustrated with this situation—Weston or her. At the moment, she thought she might be the winner.

Because they hadn't caught the Moonlight Strangler after all.

And that meant he was still out there. Maybe still plotting to kill her.

However, he hadn't tried to murder her tonight. Not yet anyway. The attacker who'd hurt Teddy and fired shots into the house wasn't old enough to be the Moonlight Strangler.

So, who was he?

Addie didn't know, but she was hoping to find out soon. The same was obviously true for Weston.

He had a death grip on the steering wheel of Addie's truck as they drove toward the hospital. She didn't miss the glares he was doling out to her, either. He clearly didn't want her on this trip with him into town. Didn't want her out in the open.

Well, Addie wasn't so thrilled about it herself, but she wouldn't have felt any safer at home than she would at the hospital, where she'd no doubt be surrounded by lawmen.

Maybe surrounded by answers, as well.

Since their attacker would soon be at the hospital, too.

The injured man was just ahead of them in an ambulance. Jericho was inside with him and the medics. Her brother would also be doling out some glares when he learned she'd disobeyed his order for her to stay put at the ranch and had instead come to the hospital with Weston.

But before Addie had left the ranch, she'd first made sure her mother had plenty of protection, both from the ranch hands, Weston's two PI friends and her other brother Chase who'd hurried out to the scene. Only then, and only after the ambulance had driven away, had Addie demanded that Weston take her with him.

She'd deal with Jericho later.

Later, she'd have to deal with a lot of things.

Including Weston's arrival.

After three months of not hearing from him, she had written him out of her life. Out of her heart, as well. Addie wasn't certain what was going on in Weston's head, but she doubted he would just disappear again.

Well, not until he had caught the Moonlight Strangler anyway.

"I should have known," Addie heard Weston say.

It wasn't the first time in the past fifteen minutes he'd said something along those same lines. And maybe they should have known that the Moonlight Strangler would send a lackey to the ranch instead of risking a personal appearance.

Especially after the killer had let Weston know that she was his next target.

Still, a lackey could have killed her just as well as the Moonlight Strangler.

"He's way too young to be the killer," Weston grumbled. He was talking to himself now. Or rather berating himself, since the next mumblings had some profanity mixed in with them.

Yes, the guy was too young. Probably only in his late twenties, judging from the quick glimpse she'd gotten of him before Jericho had demanded that she go back inside. Since the Moonlight Strangler had been murdering women for at least thirty years, the shooter definitely fell into the lackey category.

Or worse.

He could be some kind of crazed groupie who had absolutely no knowledge of the Moonlight Strangler's identity. This could all have been some kind of a sick hoax.

One that could have gotten a lot of people killed.

They were lucky that hadn't happened, but they weren't out of the woods yet. Teddy was alive and was already en route to the hospital in an ambulance ahead of the one carrying their attacker, but Addie had no idea how serious his injuries were.

"Thank you for saving my mother and me," she told Weston.

He glanced at her, maybe wondering if she was sincere. She was. Despite the other stuff going on between Weston and her—the baby stuff—she was thankful he'd been there when the bullets had started flying.

She'd be even more thankful if she knew that was the last of the bullets. But Addie didn't think she would be that lucky.

"Is it possible this guy faked the threatening letters you got?" she asked.

"No." Weston didn't hesitate. "There were personal details in them. Like the cuts on the faces of the victims. That was never leaked to the press." But then he stopped, added more profanity. "I suppose, though, he could have sent the last two letters. The one that threatened you and my sister. Still..."

"What?" she pressed when he didn't continue.

"They felt real." His mouth tightened as if disgusted that he'd rely on something like feelings, but Addie didn't dismiss it.

"Maybe they felt real because my birth father told him exactly what to write." Now it was her turn to mumble some profanity. If that was the case, then they needed this slimebag lackey to talk, to tell them anything and everything he might know about the Moonlight Strangler.

"Are you okay?" Weston asked a moment later.

Addie didn't miss his glance that landed on her stomach. She wasn't okay, not by a long shot. She felt raw and bruised as if she'd gone through a physical attack instead of just the threat of one. The sound of those bullets would stay with her for the rest of her life.

"I'm fine," she settled for saying. And she hoped that was true. Her precious baby didn't deserve to go through this. No one did.

"You should see a doctor while you're at the hospital. Just to make sure," he added.

His tone made it sound like an order. Which made her rethink her notion that he'd just leave after catching her birth father.

No.

She really didn't want to have to deal with this on top of everything else.

"For the record, we barely know each other," Addie tossed out there. "And you won't exactly be welcome in my family."

Another glance at her stomach. "Is that supposed to send me running for the hills?"

"It might after you meet Jericho."

"I've already met Jericho," he countered.

"Barely." They'd exchanged brief introductions and some testosterone-laced glares while waiting for the ambulance. "He's very protective of me."

Especially since he'd learned she was pregnant. Addie was thankful for his brotherly love. Thankful for all the other things he'd done for her, including offering her a shoulder when she'd been crying over her heart-crushing encounter with Weston. But Jericho wouldn't be showing much love to the man who'd slept with his kid sister and then dumped her.

"I'll deal with Jericho," Weston said as if it were gospel.

"Good luck with that," she said in the same tone he'd used.

Still behind the ambulance, he pulled her truck into the parking lot. The very truck that he'd insisted on driving from the ranch to the hospital. Normally, that wasn't a task Addie would have just surrendered, but the truth was, she was shaking, and the nerves were still there right at the surface.

Unlike Weston's nerves.

He just seemed riled that he hadn't been able to bring all of this to a close tonight. And it still might happen. If they could get some info from the shooter.

He took the parking space nearest the ER doors. "Stay close to me and move fast," he instructed.

She spotted the two night deputies already there. Both were positioned just outside the ER. Both with their hands over their guns. A reminder that this nightmare wasn't over.

"Search anyone who tries to get in," Weston told them, and he flashed his badge.

Weston used his own body to shelter her while they made the short trek into the hospital. They were just behind Jericho and the medics, who rushed in with their patient. She didn't hear what Jericho said to the nurse at the reception desk, but Addie didn't miss the scowl he gave her when he spotted her. He came toward her just as Weston pulled her away from the doors and to the far side of the room.

Maybe just to get her away from the glass doors.

Maybe so he could make this showdown with Jericho semiprivate.

"You should be home," Jericho insisted, and in the same breath he added to Weston, "And the two of us need to *talk*." Weston was on the receiving end of an even worse scowl than she'd gotten.

She seriously doubted Jericho had only talking on his mind, and that's why Addie stepped between them. "I can handle this myself."

All right, that didn't exactly cool the fire in

Jericho's eyes. Nor did it stop Weston from moving her so that he was facing her brother head-on.

Jericho's index finger landed against Weston's chest. "You deserve to have your butt kicked for what you did to my sister. Now the question is—are you going to do something about it?"

"Yeah, I do deserve a butt-kicking," Weston readily admitted. "And Addie deserves some answers, but we can work that out later. Agreed?"

She wasn't sure Jericho would agree to anything right now, but he finally huffed, pulled her into his arms and brushed a kiss on Addie's forehead. "Are you okay? And I want the truth."

"I'll be fine," Addie assured him and stayed a moment in his arms. He might be the most stubborn brother in the universe, but he'd walk through fire for her. And vice versa.

"I already told her I want the doctor to check her out just in case," Weston insisted.

Jericho made a sound of agreement.

"I can think for myself," she reminded both of them.

But she was talking to the air because both of them ignored her. Jericho motioned for them to follow him, and he led them into a private waiting room just up the hall.

No windows, thank goodness. She figured it'd take a lifetime or two before she walked past one and didn't hear the sound of bullets shattering glass.

Weston tipped his head to the wallet her brother had in his left hand. "Does that belong to the shooter?"

It was clear her brother didn't want to drop the personal part of this conversation with Weston, but she saw the moment he shifted from big brother to lawman. "Yes. My brother Jax is running a background check on him, but we know his name is Lonny Ogden. He's thirty-one and lives in San Antonio."

Addie repeated it to see if it rang any bells. It didn't. "You're sure that's his real name?"

"The photo on the license matches the one at DMV. I'm running his prints just to verify, but on the drive over, I had Jax check on Ogden's rap sheet." Jericho paused, scrubbed his hand over his face and gave a weary sigh. "He doesn't have one. Ogden's never been arrested."

Hard to believe that the man who'd just tried to kill her had never been in trouble with the law.

"Ogden had a cell phone on him, and I had a ranch hand deliver it to Jax at the station. Jax'll examine the calls and any other phone records Ogden might have left."

"Did Ogden say why he did this?" Weston asked.

Another weary sigh from Jericho. "He rambled

on a lot, not much of it making sense. When I asked him if he was working for the Moonlight Strangler, he said no, that he was working for a higher being that didn't live on this planet."

Now it was Addie's turn to sigh. "He's insane."

"Possibly. Or he could be faking it." Jericho's gaze came back to hers. "He said he couldn't have the Moonlight Strangler's blood live on and that you weren't doing all you could to help the cops catch the killer."

Good God. Addie had known right from the start that this attack was aimed at her, but it was sickening to hear the motive spelled out.

Well, if it was true.

"What exactly does Ogden believe I should be doing to help the cops?" Addie asked.

"It doesn't matter what he thinks. He's crazy," Weston reminded her.

That didn't make her feel any better. Mainly because it was coming from Weston. Yes, he'd saved her life, but Addie reminded herself that he'd also used her to find the Moonlight Strangler, the very monster at the heart of all of this.

"Ogden said you should try hypnosis and some drug therapy," Jericho finally answered.

"I've done both." A reminder that wasn't necessary since her brother and Weston already knew that. If she thought more hypnosis would help, she'd gladly repeat it. Ditto for another round of drug therapy once the baby was born.

"Ogden believes you know plenty of things you're not saying because you want to protect your birth father," Jericho added. "And remember that part about him being crazy."

Addie wanted to curse. Or scream. "I wouldn't protect him. Not ever." Of course, she hadn't needed to tell Jericho that. But it did make her wonder. "Is this personal for Ogden? Maybe the Moonlight Strangler killed someone he loved?"

Even though Weston wasn't touching her, she could almost feel his muscles tightening.

"We'll check all angles," Jericho assured her, but anything else he was about to say was cut off when they spotted a tall gray-haired man in scrubs making his ways toward him.

Addie instantly recognized him. It was Dr. Applewhite. There were only a handful of regular doctors at the small hospital, and she'd known Dr. Applewhite since she was in elementary school. However, she didn't usually see such a serious expression on his grandfatherly face.

"Teddy's in surgery," the doctor said right off. "He's lost a lot of blood. *A lot*," he emphasized. "But there doesn't seem to be any damage to his vital organs. He should pull through."

Addie hadn't even realized she was holding her breath until the air rushed from her throat. Like the doctor, she'd known Teddy most of her life, and it felt like a stab to the heart to know he'd been hurt because of her.

"Thanks for telling us," Addie said. "My mother's already called his family to let them know. They'll be here soon."

The doctor had no sooner stepped away when Jericho's phone buzzed, and she saw Jax's name on the screen. She also saw the debate Jericho had with himself before he finally put the call on speaker.

"I found something," Jax greeted.

Addie had braced herself for bad news, but the relief flooded through her. Guarded relief anyway.

"I'm looking at Lonny Ogden's phone records, and he's only been in contact with one person in the past twenty-four hours. Ira Canales."

Yet another name Addie didn't recognize, and apparently she wasn't the only one who didn't.

"Who is he?" Weston and Jericho asked in unison.

"He's the campaign manager for Alton Gregory Boggs."

Addie shook her head. "The attorney who's running for the state senate?"

"The very one," Jax confirmed.

She'd seen campaign ads. Everyone probably had. Pictures of a smiling Boggs and his equally smiling wife were plastered on billboards all over the area.

"It's not just a couple of calls to Canales," Jax went on. "Ogden phoned him six times today. All under a minute long so I can't be sure if Canales actually spoke with him. Ogden could have just left him messages."

True, but it was a start. Maybe Ogden had said something to Canales that would tell them if Ogden truly had a connection to the Moonlight Strangler. *Any* connection that would help them learn the killer's identity.

"I'll call Canales now and have him come in tomorrow," Jax continued. "Jericho, have you been able to question Ogden yet?"

But Jericho didn't get a chance to answer because of the shouts that were coming from the ER. One of the shouts she instantly recognized as coming from the night deputy, Dexter Conway.

"Stop!" Dexter yelled.

"Stay here," Jericho insisted. He drew his gun, then hesitated a split second so he could make eye contact with Weston. "Watch out for her."

Jericho rushed out, racing toward the sounds of Dexter's repeated shouts for someone or something to stop. Weston stepped in the doorway in front of her, and he, too, drew his gun.

Just like that her heart was right back in her throat. "What's happening?"

Weston shook his head.

But Addie heard something she definitely hadn't wanted to hear.

A gunshot.

The sound put her heart right back in her throat. "Another attack?" she managed to ask.

"Maybe." Weston didn't budge. He kept watch and then started a new round of profanity. "Yeah. It's a gunman. And Jericho's in pursuit."

## *Chapter Six*

This day had gone about as bad as Weston could have imagined, and sadly it wasn't over yet.

Not with a hired gun on the loose.

And judging from the fact that Jericho hadn't called Addie and Weston yet, the sheriff and deputies had yet to apprehend the armed man who'd tried to get into the hospital. The same man who'd taken a shot at one of the deputies when he'd tried to question him.

With both Addie and Ogden in the hospital at that time, there was no way to know which one was the intended target.

But the thug had definitely had a target all right.

The deputy had reported that the man had been armed to the hilt and had tried to strong-arm his way into the hospital after the deputy stopped him for questioning. Too bad the guy had managed to run off before they could learn who he was after and who'd sent him.

That wasn't something Weston wanted to learn the hard way.

And that's why he'd insisted on bringing Addie back to her family's ranch. A plan heartily endorsed by her brothers. However, it was temporary. Well, it was unless they managed to figure out the identity of a killer who'd been eluding the police and FBI for three decades.

Yeah, this bad day definitely wasn't over yet.

Weston finished his latest call with one of his Ranger friends, and he turned around knowing Addie would be right there in the ranch's kitchen. Waiting for news. What he hadn't figured was that *right there* was close enough that he bumped into her. He automatically reached for her.

Not a good idea.

Because she stepped back as if he'd scalded her.

Weston couldn't blame her. He'd gotten her pregnant, walked out on her, and here he'd been back in her life for only a couple of hours and someone had already tried to kill her. Worse, he couldn't even guarantee her that things would get better.

"Anything on the guy who got away?" she asked.

"No." But she might have already known the answer since she'd perhaps been standing close enough to hear his conversation. "I've asked the Rangers to assist with the search."

"Are you on good enough terms with them to ask that?"

Barely.

Weston kept that to himself and nodded. Most of his fellow officers thought he'd crossed a line between obsession and justice when it came to finding Collette's killer.

There were days, and nights, like this one when Weston had to agree with them.

"They'll find him," Weston assured her. At best that was wishful thinking. At worst, a lie. But he hated that look of worry on her face.

A face he could hardly see because all the overhead lights were off. But the Christmas lights were twinkling and shimmering outside the windows.

The lack of inside lights, even here in the kitchen, was a precaution in case a shooter managed to get past a wall of security that Weston had established with ranch hands, PIs and deputies—all on the ranch grounds to make sure Addie was safe.

She moved back to the counter, finished off a glass of milk and then studied him. "Would you still use me to draw out the killer?"

A reasonable question since several hours ago, that's exactly what he'd planned to do. "No. I'll have to think of another way."

One that didn't involve endangering the baby she was carrying.

Or her.

Yes, Addie herself was playing into this now. Weston could blame the blasted attraction for that. It was still there, just as it had been when he'd first laid eyes on her.

"So…that means you'll be leaving," she added. And it didn't exactly have a "please stay" tone attached to it.

"I'll stay until Jericho gets home." Whenever that would be. The sheriff was no doubt up to his ears in alligators.

"And then?" she pressed.

That was the million-dollar question. He didn't even have a fifty-cent answer. "Well, I won't be leaving for good. I'll be part of the baby's life."

"I don't expect that from you."

"You should." Weston tried to rein in the anger he heard in his voice. "Despite what you think of me, I'm not some dirtbag who'll run out on his own child. On any child for that matter."

"Oh." That was all Addie said for a long time. "So…you've always wanted children?"

"No." He didn't have to think about that, but he did have to consider how to explain it. "I always figured I wouldn't pass on my DNA to an innocent child. Let's just say my parents weren't stellar and leave it at that."

Her eyebrow lifted. "I think I've got you beat hands down in the bad DNA department. Were either of them notorious serial killers who wanted to murder you?"

He had to shake his head on that one.

She made a yeah-I-got-you-beat sound. "As far as I'm concerned, their DNA has nothing to do with this child." She slid her hand over her stomach. "After all, even with our bad blood, we didn't turn out so wrong."

The jury was still out on that when it came to him. Weston wasn't sure he could forgive himself for what he'd done to Addie.

Or Collette.

Nor was he sure he wanted their forgiveness.

He deserved this private hell he was living.

Addie paused again, glanced around. "Then I suppose we'll work out some kind of custody agreement. Something simple and nice that doesn't involve tempers flaring and such."

That was good, but it didn't ring true, and it felt as if someone had just scraped their nails on a chalkboard. Maybe it was that irritation or the events of the night. Heck, maybe he had indeed lost it, but Weston hooked his arm around her waist, pulled her to him and kissed her.

He'd meant for it to be a reminder that flaring tempers were the least of their worries. And that any agreement would be far from simple or nice.

But one taste of her, and Weston got a lesson of his own.

Best not to play with fire.

And that's exactly what he was doing whenever he was within breathing distance of Addie.

It was a short-lived disaster. However, it still packed a wallop. Addie pushed herself away from him and looked ready to knock him into the middle of the next county.

"Don't," she managed to say. She even managed a glare before she cursed. "I won't make the mistake of sleeping with you again."

"Good." And he was reasonably sure he meant that. "Because right now, we don't need this kind of distraction."

"This kind of *distraction* isn't ever going to happen again," she clarified. And she was probably sure that she meant it, too.

Thankfully, they didn't have to deal with this mental foreplay any longer because Weston's phone dinged, and he spotted a text from Jax on the screen.

"Ogden's out of surgery," Weston read aloud so Addie wouldn't have to move closer to him to read it. "He lawyered up."

It was exactly what Weston had expected him to do since the idiot was facing multiple counts of attempted murder. Still, he might be willing to cut some kind of deal to give them info about anyone he might be working with.

Including Ira Canales.

Weston definitely wanted to be at the sheriff's office in the morning for that interview.

"Come on," Weston told her. "You need to get some rest." That wasn't just coming from him, either. The doctor had insisted on it when he'd examined her while they were at the hospital.

Addie stepped around him, careful not to brush against him. It didn't help. Weston could still feel her in his arms. Could still see images of her naked.

Yeah, that really didn't help.

It also didn't help that he was following her to her bedroom. He wouldn't go in the room with her, of course, but he would end up sleeping nearby. With Addie so close that he could remember that mistake of a kiss he'd just made.

"Jericho's going to insist on putting me in a safe house, isn't he?" she asked as they walked up the stairs.

"Probably. And if he doesn't, I will. And don't you dare say it's safe here, because the bullet holes in your office prove otherwise."

That earned him a huff. "Look, I'm not stupid. I want me and my baby to be safe. But I do a lot of things to help keep this ranch running, and I can't do those things if I'm locked away in a safe house."

"It's not permanent." Weston hoped.

She threw open the door to her bedroom and whirled around as if the argument might continue. It didn't. Addie just stared at him.

"You were in love with Collette?" she asked.

Well, that came out of the blue. And he was certain this wasn't a conversation he wanted to have. Weston settled for a nod.

"I'm trying to justify in my mind why you did what you did in San Antonio," Addie clarified.

"You can't justify that," he assured her.

"But you can." Those words hung in the air like knives over his head.

"I owed Collette. And I let her down." Weston figured that would be enough poking at old wounds tonight.

Apparently not.

"You owed her?" Addie's forehead bunched up. "What does that mean?"

Weston opened his mouth. Groaned. "It means you should climb into bed and get some rest."

As answers went, it sucked, but he was already too raw, too drained to take this bad trip down memory lane.

She stared at him several moments longer. Waiting for something he wasn't going to give her. Addie must have finally realized that because she went into her room and shut the door. She even locked it.

Good.

He didn't want her to trust him, and if Collette were still alive, she would agree.

Weston looked up the hall to make sure Iris's door was still shut. It was. Addie's mom had gone there shortly after they'd gotten back from the hospital, and maybe she would stay put until morning. He doubted she'd get much sleep. None of them would. But he didn't want either Addie or her mom wandering around the house where they could be sniper targets.

With his back against the wall, Weston eased himself to a sitting position on the floor. No doubt where he'd end up spending the night, but that was okay.

A penance of sorts.

He'd been a fool to come here and think he could fix things, that he could make Addie feel safe. Instead, he'd flamed a fire—several of them in fact.

Weston closed his eyes, praying for a quick nap. Didn't happen. His phone rang, and he saw Jericho's name on the screen.

"Did you find the hired gun?" Weston greeted.

"Yeah."

It wasn't an answer Weston had been expecting. He figured on getting another dose of bad news.

Then, he realized Jericho's silence probably meant that was still to come.

"I followed him to the old abandoned hospital outside of town," Jericho continued. "He drew on me, and I had to kill him."

Hell. They needed the guy alive so he could talk. "Did he have any ID?"

"No, but he had some pictures on him that made it pretty clear who he was targeting."

"He was sent to kill Ogden," Weston concluded, "before he could tell us anything."

"No. I wish." Jericho paused again, then cursed. "His target was Addie."

# *Chapter Seven*

Addie thought a maximum security prison might have fewer safety measures than she had at the moment.

Weston, Jericho and three deputies. Plus the two PIs and two more armed ranch hands who'd followed Weston and her on the drive from the ranch to the sheriff's office. They were waiting outside as if they were about to be blasted to smithereens.

She didn't mind the protection. Not for her sake but for the baby's.

But there was something all of these lawmen weren't telling her.

Jax kept dodging her gaze. The other deputies, too. And more than usual, Jericho was scowling along with looking more intimidating. Of course, Jericho didn't just look intimating.

He was.

Yet, Weston seemed to match him in that department.

Maybe it had something to do with the fact that

both had probably gotten very little sleep and were on edge. Jericho had spent the night at the sheriff's office, and Weston had stayed right outside her door. All night. She should probably be happy that he was showing such an interest in keeping her safe, but having him around was a reminder she didn't need.

Like that kiss.

Her brain was telling her this was a man she shouldn't trust. Not with her heart anyway. He seemed to be doing a better than average job protecting her body. But that kiss was a reminder to guard her feelings. She wasn't sure she could survive another to have her heart broken by Weston a second time.

Worse, she wasn't sure if he had any immediate plans to leave anytime soon.

In the wee hours of the morning, he'd had someone deliver several changes of clothes to the ranch. And Weston had moved those things into the guest room across from hers. He'd also had several phone conversations with Jericho. About what, she didn't know, but Addie was about to find out.

"You're hardheaded," Jericho said to her the moment he finished a phone call. He came out from behind his desk and made a beeline toward her. "You should have stayed at the ranch."

"He's right," Weston agreed. Probably the only

thing Weston and her brother actually agreed about. "There was no need for you to be here for Canales's and Boggs's interviews."

Oh, yes, there was. Especially for Canales, since the injured shooter had been in phone contact with the campaign manager. Of course, Weston had tried to talk her out of it. He'd failed.

"Boggs did say he wanted to see you," Jax volunteered.

It took Addie a moment to realize he was talking to her. "Me? Why? I don't know him."

Jax lifted his shoulder. "When I asked Boggs to come in for the interview, he wanted to know if you'd be here. I said no, probably not. And he said that was too bad because he wanted to meet you."

She hoped this wasn't another case of someone wanting to meet her because of her biological father. There were some strange people out there with fascinations about serial killers.

"What time are Canales and Boggs coming in?" Weston asked.

Jericho checked his watch. "Should be any minute now. After that, I want Addie back at the ranch."

Huffing, she got in her brother's face. "Tell me what's going on," Addie said, glancing first at Jericho then Weston.

Weston and Jericho did some glance-exchanges

of their own. "The hit man who showed up at the hospital last night—he was after you."

All right. That was a truth that punched her a little harder than expected. Of course, she'd known Ogden had wanted her dead, but now this thug had wanted that, too.

"You're sure?" she asked, but immediately waved off the question. They were certain, and it explained all the extra security.

Jericho led her to his office. The first thing she spotted on his cluttered desk was a photo. A photo of *her*. It was a grainy shot that looked as if it'd been taken through a long-range lens.

"Did you know you'd been photographed?" Weston asked.

She shook her head. Hadn't had a clue. Which made this even more sickening. How long had this monster been following her? Or maybe it was more than one monster, since the person who'd taken that photo could have given it to the hit man so he'd be sure he was killing the right person.

Her stomach clenched.

"We got an ID on the dead guy around midnight," Jericho continued. "Curtis Nicks. Unlike Ogden, he's got a record, and the FBI got into his computer. There were more photos of you, but this appears to be the only one he printed out."

Because he only needed one.

But there was something else. She didn't ask

Jericho what that was. Instead, she turned to Weston and motioned for him to continue. "I'm sure in one of those many conversations you had with Jericho, you know everything that's going on."

He made a sound to confirm that but took his time answering. "Nicks has a file on his computer with the address to the ranch and some other notes. The file was new, created just yesterday." Weston paused, met her eye-to-eye. "If Nicks hadn't been able to get to you, he planned to use your family to draw you out."

"Oh, God." Her knees buckled, and if Weston hadn't caught her, she would have fallen. He had her sit in the chair next to Jericho's desk. "Mom," she managed to say.

"I'm sending her to her sister's place," Jericho quickly volunteered. Addie's aunt had two sons, both cops, who lived with her, so that was a good first step.

"But what about you?" she asked. "And Jax, Chase?"

"All of us are taking precautions. We've even got someone on Teddy while he's recovering at the hospital. Ditto for Weston's sister. The Rangers have beefed up security for her, too."

Good. Addie didn't want anyone else hurt. Especially anyone connected to Weston. Her birth father had already cost him enough.

Jericho's phone buzzed, and he scowled when he looked at the screen. "I have to take this. Stay with her," he added to Weston.

"You heard what your brother said." Weston pulled up the chair and sat so they were face-to-face. "Everyone's taking precautions."

Addie wasn't sure that'd be enough. "Is Nicks even connected to the Moonlight Strangler?"

"He appears to be. He mentions him in his notes. Not by name, just the initials MS."

Great. Now the Moonlight Strangler was hiring hit men to come after her.

"What about Ogden?" she asked. "Is he saying anything?"

"Not to any of us, but according to Jax, his lawyer was with him most of the night. Not a cheap attorney, either. This guy is top-shelf. Jax is following the money trail to see if anyone's paying for those round-the-clock legal services."

Good. Maybe that would lead to something.

"So, maybe Ogden wasn't connected to the other hit man who came to the hospital," Addie said, thinking out loud.

"Maybe. But two armed men in the same night probably isn't a coincidence. That's why you'll need to go to a safe house," Weston added. "The marshals can set one up for you."

Twenty-four hours ago, she would have nixed the idea. Not now, though. Because Weston was right.

She was about to tell Weston to start the arrangements, but Addie got to her feet when she heard voices in the main squad room. She immediately saw Jericho greeting two men. One she recognized from the billboards.

Alton Boggs.

He wasn't a big man, only about five-eight, and he looked more like a 1940s film star than a former rancher. His black hair was slicked back. Teeth perfectly white and straight. His gaze shifted over the room until it landed on her. Only then did he smile, and it wasn't the sort of welcoming smile, either. It was as if he was trying to reassure her.

Or something.

The man with the salt-and-pepper hair who stepped in behind Boggs was at least half a foot taller. No smile for him. His mouth was pulled into what appeared to be a permanent frown. He barely spared her a glance. His attention instead went to Jericho.

"Sheriff Crockett," Canales said, the impatience dripping from his voice. "I hope to resolve this fast. Mr. Boggs has a fund-raising luncheon in San Antonio, and we need to get back on the road."

Boggs, however, showed no such impatience. He came closer to her, extending his hand for her to shake. "Addie Crockett. Your pictures don't do you justice."

She actually dropped back a step, and Weston moved in between Boggs and her. Only then did Boggs seem to realize he'd made her uncomfortable.

"Alton Boggs," he said, extending his hand to Weston.

"Weston Cade."

"Ah, yes, the Texas Ranger," Boggs provided.

Weston lifted his eyebrow, questioning how the man knew that.

"I see I need to explain," Boggs said. "Is there someplace we can all talk *privately*?" he asked Weston. "I'd like Addie to hear what I have to say, as well."

Jericho didn't jump to answer, but he finally tipped his head toward the hall and led them into an interview room.

"There's no need to get into all of this," Canales said to his boss. "The sheriff only wants me to explain why that idiot in the hospital called me."

"What do you mean by all of *this*?" Addie asked.

Boggs drew in a long breath and sank down into one of the chairs. He motioned for her to do the same and didn't continue until she had. "I've been trying to catch the Moonlight Strangler for years, and when I heard about your DNA connection, I'd hoped he would try to contact you. Has he?"

She groaned. "You're a groupie?"

"Hardly. Your father murdered one of my childhood friends, Cora McGee."

The name was familiar to Addie, as were all the victims. "*Birth* father. And I'm sorry."

"No need to apologize for anything he did. But you understand now why I was interested in you."

Weston and she exchanged uneasy glances. "Convince me why you were really interested." Weston insisted.

"You're obviously a skeptic. That probably comes with the badge. Well, I was interested in you as well since you, too, lost a loved one to the Moonlight Strangler," Boggs added.

"How did you know who I was?" Weston asked.

"I've made it a point to know anyone and everyone associated with the case. Clearly, so have you." Boggs stopped on the last syllable. "Or are you here in Appaloosa Pass because Addie and you are...*together*?"

Addie felt the goose bumps shiver over her skin. She had no intention of answering him, but Weston had a different notion.

"We're not together, not like that," Weston snapped.

Only then did she remember the killer's threat, that if she and Weston teamed up, he'd murder Weston's sister. Besides, they really weren't together.

And it would be dangerous to both of them if anyone thought they were.

"The only reason Weston is here," she said, "is because he wants to catch the Moonlight Strangler, too."

Boggs studied them a moment as if trying to figure out if that was true, and he finally nodded. "Of course. I just assumed it because you're two attractive people. But I can see I was wrong about that."

"There's no reason to get into any of this," Canales interrupted. He checked his watch again. "But to answer your question about this Lonny Ogden, I have no idea why he phoned me, because I didn't answer his calls. I'm sure the phone records will show that."

"They do," Jericho verified. "But that doesn't mean you don't know Ogden or know why he was calling."

"I don't know him." Canales's mouth tightened even more. "Plenty of people call me about the campaign. Heck, for all I know he could have been hired by one of Alton's opponents to sully his name."

"Maybe," Weston said, taking the seat next to Addie. "You still haven't convinced me. Maybe Ogden knew about your boss's connection to the Moonlight Strangler?"

"That's exactly the kind of talk I'm trying to stop," Canales snapped. "This will be a tight campaign race, and I don't want anyone using a smear tactic like this. We're running on a platform of traditional values. On family. Any mention of a serial killer could taint that."

Judging from his scowl, Weston wasn't pleased with that answer, and he turned back to Boggs. "Did Ogden try to contact you, too?"

"All my nonpersonal calls go through him these days." He aimed a glance at Canales. "So it's possible Ogden was actually trying to get in touch with me. It's also possible it was about the Moonlight Strangler." He paused, studied Addie again. "Has your father ever contacted you through a call or letters?"

Because Weston's arm was touching hers, she felt him tense. "No letters," she answered. And waited for Boggs to continue.

"Well, he might have sent me some," Boggs finally said.

It got very quiet in the room. For a couple of seconds anyway.

"Excuse me?" Jericho snarled. "What letters?"

Boggs held up his hands in a keep-calm gesture. "They might not even be real, but I started getting them a few months ago, and he said he was the Moonlight Strangler. Always signed them MS."

She looked at Weston to see if that matched the ones he'd received, and he nodded.

"What's in the letters?" she asked.

Boggs took another deep breath. "He doesn't

say anything about the murders. He just keeps asking me if I remember him. I don't," he quickly volunteered. "But apparently he thinks we met years ago."

"Did you?" Weston sounded very much like a lawman right now. A riled one.

"No. Maybe," Boggs amended. "I'm sixty-one. I've met a lot of people, and it's my guess that he saw one of my campaign ads and latched on to me."

"He gets letters like that all the time," Canales added. "Some are nutcases who just want to be connected with someone famous. If we turned all of them over the police, the cops wouldn't have time to do their jobs."

"I want those letters," Weston insisted.

Boggs quickly nodded. "Of course. I'll have someone bring them here to the sheriff's office right away." He took out his phone to make a call.

"I don't want them leaked to the press," Canales snapped to Weston. "It could hurt the election if the voters find out Boggs had any connection whatsoever to the Moonlight Strangler."

"Yeah, yeah," Jericho grumbled.

Weston stood, faced Canales. "Your campaign isn't even on my radar. I'll do whatever it takes to catch the killer and keep Addie safe."

"I'll call you back," Boggs said to the person on the other end of the line, and with his gaze fixed on Addie, he put his phone away. "Are you in danger?"

The burst of air that left her mouth wasn't from laughter. "Yes. That's why it's important to know if you ever met my birth father. I need to know who he is so he can be stopped."

Boggs nodded. "You think those letters really could be from him?"

"They could be," she settled for saying. No sense getting into the ones he'd sent Weston.

"The letters will be analyzed," Weston explained, "and I'm sure the FBI will want you to go through hypnosis or something to see if you can remember if you ever met this guy."

"Hypnosis?" Canales piped in. "That's not a good idea."

When Canales didn't explain, they all stared at him.

"I had a rough childhood," Boggs admitted. "Ira's just worried that digging up old bones might be bad for my mental state. And the campaign. People don't want to hear about a poor kid who clawed his way out of abuse and poverty. They want to see me with my beautiful wife of nearly twenty-five years and know that I stand for the same honest and upright values they stand for."

Weston added some profanity under his breath. "How bad do you think your mental state and the campaign will be if another woman is killed and you could have done something to prevent it?"

"Point taken," Boggs said, but it was clear from Canales's scowl that he didn't agree.

Boggs turned to Addie again. "I'd hoped by seeing you that I might remember if I'd ever met your father. Your *birth* father," Boggs corrected. "I thought maybe you'd look like him and that I'd recognize you or something."

"Do you?" she wanted to know.

Boggs glanced back at Canales, and for a moment she thought Canales would be able to silence his boss with the stern look he was giving him. He didn't.

"Ira, you remember I told you about the little girl that the daycare woman had for a while?" Boggs asked.

Canales didn't roll his eyes exactly, but it was close. "You don't think..." He cursed. "You think she's that kid?" He stabbed his index finger toward Addie.

That got her attention, and Addie slowly rose to her feet. Canales's question had her heart racing. Her breath, too.

"Over the years, I've talked to as many people as I could who lived within a fifty mile radius of where you were found. Because I figured your birth father had probably been in the area, too. A couple of months back, I met a woman named

Daisy," Boggs explained. "She babysat a little girl for a while."

Addie jumped right on that. "Why would you think it was me?"

"Because the age and description are right. Blond hair, big blue eyes. Like yours. I figured if you truly were that little girl and if the killer was right about me having known him, then I might remember meeting you. Might remember meeting the killer, as well. But I don't recall running into any man who looked like that child. Or like you."

"But it's possible?" she pressed.

After several long moments, Boggs nodded.

That put her right back in the chair. They might have a link, though it was a slim one. What were the odds that Boggs would have seen her as a child?

Not likely.

But if Addie had indeed been with Daisy, then the woman might be able to answer a lot of questions.

"I'll get you some water," Weston insisted.

She must look as shaken as she felt for him to make that offer. More than anything she wanted answers, but Addie was afraid those answers weren't going to be ones she liked.

Nor would the answers necessarily make this danger disappear.

Weston left the room for just a minute and returned with three paper cups of water. He gave one to her and handed the others to Canales and Boggs. Canales drank his down without stopping. Not Boggs, though. He looked at Weston, his forehead bunching up, and he put the cup on the table.

"Thanks, but I'm not thirsty," Boggs said.

"Why didn't you tell the FBI about this Daisy?" Jericho asked.

Boggs shrugged. "I wasn't sure it was connected. I'm still not sure."

Jericho took out a notepad and pen and dropped it on the table. "I want Daisy's full name and any contact information you have."

"Daisy Vogel," Boggs provided, and he stood. "I don't remember her address, but I'm sure you can find it."

Weston looked at Canales, no doubt wondering if he had more info.

"Never met the woman. I knew Alton back then, but I never crossed paths with Daisy." Canales crushed his cup and tossed it into the trash can. "Just remember, I don't want any of this backwashing onto the campaign. Are we finished here?"

"For now," Jericho answered.

That was enough to get Canales moving. "Come on, Alton. We can't be late for that fund-raiser."

"Let me know if you find Daisy." Boggs reached out as if he might touch Addie's arm, but he must have remembered her earlier reaction because instead he mumbled a goodbye and left with Canales.

"I'll see what I can do about getting Daisy's number," Jericho said to Weston, and he tipped his head to the trash can. "I'll also bring back an evidence bag to take care of that. Too bad you couldn't get Boggs to take the bait."

"Bait?" Addie repeated, turning to Weston when her brother walked out.

Weston shrugged. "I wanted their DNA so we can compare it."

Addie felt her eyes widen. "You think one of them might be the Moonlight Strangler?"

"They fit the profile."

That stalled her breath in her throat.

"Are you okay?" Weston asked.

She nodded. She was getting good at lying. Or so she thought. Weston saw right through her.

"We just need to be sure," he added. He slid his arm around her waist. Not a hug exactly. But close.

All right, it was a hug.

And Addie couldn't help herself. She leaned against him.

Had she really just been face-to-face with her birth father?

"I thought maybe I'd feel something if I ever

saw him," she said. "Maybe some kind of genetic memory connection."

"You're not like him. You probably won't feel anything like that at all."

But she would feel *something.* So would Weston. Especially since her birth father had murdered Collette.

"Will you ever be able to look at me, at the baby, and not think of Collette and her killer?" Addie wanted to snatch back the question as soon as she asked it. But it was too late.

"I don't think of them when I look at you," he said as if choosing his words carefully. "Trust me, that's not a good thing. Because it means I'm losing focus. And that might be dangerous for all of us."

Addie heard the footsteps in the hall, and she stepped away from Weston. But not before Jericho saw them. He scowled, of course. Probably because he thought she was on her way to another broken heart.

She wasn't.

Once the danger was over, she would put some emotional distance between herself and Weston.

"I got Daisy Vogel's home phone number," Jericho announced. "She has no record. Not even a parking ticket, and she's lived at the same place for the past forty years. I thought you'd want to listen in while I try to call her."

Addie nodded. "I do."

She held her breath, watching Jericho press in the numbers. He put the call on speaker and waited. They didn't have to wait long. A woman answered on the second ring.

"Daisy Vogel?" Jericho asked.

"Yes. And according to my caller ID, you're Jericho Crockett."

"That's right. I'm the sheriff in Appaloosa Pass. I wanted to ask you a few questions about a case I'm working on."

"Crockett," Daisy repeated, obviously ignoring Jericho's response. "You live on the Appaloosa Pass Ranch?"

"I do—"

"Is your adopted sister there with you?" Daisy interrupted.

Weston and Jericho looked as if they were debating the answer they'd give her, but Addie solved that for them.

"I'm here," Addie answered.

Silence. For a long time.

"Good." Though it didn't sound as if Daisy actually thought it was good. "The Crocketts named you Addie, right?"

"They did." And Addie waited through yet another long silence.

"I figured you'd eventually find your way to

me," Daisy finally continued. "I knew sooner or later you'd find out."

Addie had to take a deep breath before she could ask the next question. "Find out what?"

Daisy took a deep breath, as well. "If you want some answers about your past, come and see me. Because I know who you really are."

# *Chapter Eight*

As ideas went, this one was *bad.* Weston was sure of it.

But he couldn't see another way around it. Daisy had refused to say more on the phone, and after Jericho had called her back twice, the woman had hung up on him and hadn't answered any other calls.

Maybe Daisy had simply wanted to talk to Addie face-to-face, and this wasn't some kind of trap to lure Addie into the open. However, Weston had seen a lot of things as a lawman, and he wasn't about to trust some woman claiming to have information.

*I know who you really are*, Daisy had told Addie.

Well, he'd see about that.

Ditto for Jericho, who was behind the wheel of the cruiser. In the front seat with him, Jericho had brought along Mack Parkman, one of the other deputies, just in case this bad idea went even further south. The cruiser was bullet-resistant, and with three lawmen around her, Addie stood a good chance of being safe.

But a *chance* was far from being 100 percent.

According to the GPS, Daisy lived forty miles from Appaloosa Pass, and they were already halfway there. However, Daisy's place wasn't exactly on the beaten path. She lived on a farm road in an old house that'd belonged to her late husband, who'd been dead for nearly thirty years. About the same amount of time the Moonlight Strangler had been killing.

Weston hoped that wasn't some kind of weird coincidence.

"I don't remember any woman named Daisy," Addie insisted. She was leaning her head against the window, her eyes partly closed as if she were trying to coax those old memories into returning.

"You were three years old, maybe younger. Of course you won't remember her."

But the FBI would no doubt want to test that notion. The other times they'd hypnotized Addie and used drug therapy on her, they'd been specifically trying to get her to recall memories of the Moonlight Strangler. Now they would want to repeat that while pressing her about Daisy.

"This is a long shot anyway," Weston went on. "If Daisy really knew something about your past, then why hasn't she already come forward? Especially once it was leaked that you're the Moonlight Strangler's biological daughter."

Addie made a sound of agreement. Then she paused. "Unless she thought he would kill her. Which he might."

Weston couldn't dismiss that, and if Daisy turned out to be legit, the woman was in serious danger.

Jericho must have caught some part of that conversation because he glanced back at them using the rearview mirror. But it was just a glance, and he returned to the call he was on with the crime lab.

"Boggs or Canales might not keep quiet about Daisy," Addie added under her breath.

"Canales will." Weston couldn't say the same for Boggs, though. "Canales is more worried about the campaign than the investigation. Or your safety."

"Yes." She drew in a long breath, repeated her response. "And I might know soon if he's my birth father." She lifted her head, looked at him. "But what about Boggs? You didn't get his DNA."

No, and Boggs had seemed pretty darn suspicious when Weston had brought that cup of water into the interview room. Not Canales, though. Maybe because Canales had nothing to hide. Or perhaps he just hadn't realized that Weston hadn't served him the water out of the goodness of his heart.

"There'll be other opportunities to get Boggs's DNA," Weston told her.

And maybe Daisy would tell them something—anything—that they could use to get a court order for the DNA test. Of course, with Boggs's connections, money and reputation, it was going to take a lot to force him to contribute his DNA for a murder investigation.

"Jericho's running Ogden's DNA, too," he added. "Ogden's too young to be the Moonlight Strangler, but Jericho thought maybe Ogden might have a record under an alias."

At least that's the explanation Jericho had given Weston. Maybe that's all there was to it. But it was possible Jericho had reasons he wasn't willing to share with him. With anybody just yet. It made Weston wonder—did Jericho believe Ogden had some kind of blood connection to the Moonlight Strangler?

"Jericho isn't scowling at you as much as he was," she whispered after glancing at her brother. Jericho was so involved in his conversation that he didn't seem to hear her. Neither did Deputy Parkman, who was making his own calls, trying to get more background info on Daisy.

"Should I be worried about Jericho's lack of scowls?" Weston was only partly serious.

They shared a very short, weary smile. "We both should be. Does he know the Moonlight Strangler warned us about teaming up?"

"I told him. I arranged to have copies of all the letters sent to the sheriff's office. Just like Boggs. Maybe together they'll give us clues that we don't already have."

"Maybe," Addie said, not sounding very hopeful. "Jericho's convinced we'll find the killer soon. After that, don't be surprised if he tries to pressure you into marrying me."

Weston hadn't meant to hesitate, but he did, and that hesitation got Addie's attention.

She huffed. "He's already talked to you about it."

"It came up in conversation. But probably not like you think. Jericho doesn't believe I'm good enough for you. Because I lied to you about who I was. Because I left you."

Though he probably hadn't needed to clarify that for her.

"And there's that part about my being the target of a serial killer," she added. "One who murdered the woman you loved." Addie leaned forward, making eye contact with him. "For the record, I'm not getting married just because I'm pregnant." She shot a glare at her brother, who didn't seem to be listening. "I can raise this baby just fine without a wedding ring."

"Jericho said something along those same lines." Actually, it was exactly along those lines.

"Well, good." She sounded surprised that she and her brother were on the same page.

But they weren't on the same page with Weston.

"Your birth father might not even know you're pregnant," Weston explained. "And if he did, he might back off."

Addie stared at him with her mouth slightly open. "Is that some kind of argument for a big public announcement to tell everyone that in about six months we'll be parents?"

The parent label mentally threw him for a moment. So had the comment about her birth father killing the woman he loved.

That always felt like a twist of the knife.

But Weston pushed both aside and continued. "He wouldn't have to know the baby is mine. But I think your pregnancy should somehow make it to the press."

She stayed quiet a moment. "I don't want him to know. It makes me sick to think he has any connection whatsoever to this baby. Besides, he warned you about us teaming up."

"We won't present ourselves as a team. In fact, we can make sure everyone notices the tension between us. Which shouldn't be hard."

Since the tension was there for anyone to see.

She paused so long again that Weston was certain she was about to tell him no. But she finally nodded. "I don't suppose it could hurt. Besides, it won't be a secret for much longer. My jeans are already too tight."

Of course he had to look. Because he was stupid and male.

And, of course, he noticed her jeans were indeed tight. But not in a bad kind of way. Addie's curves had attracted him the first time he saw her, and they were still attracting him now.

Weston was thankful that the GPS interrupted his gawking with instructions to take the next road. The moment Jericho made the turn, the house came into view. No way could they miss it because it was literally sitting in the middle of some pecan trees and pasture and was the only house in sight.

As places went, it wasn't the worst for security. The tall pecans weren't that wide, so a gunman couldn't use them to hide. He spotted only one vehicle, an old truck with blistered red paint. There was a barn, but it was a good fifty yards from the house. The barn doors were wide open, and he could see clear through to the other side. If a gunman was in there, then he was in the shadows.

Something Weston would be looking for.

In fact, Weston was looking so hard for possible security problems that he didn't immediately notice Addie's reaction. Addie pulled back her shoulders. Pulled in her breath, too.

"Are you okay?" he asked. "Did you remember something?"

She shook her head. "No." Addie tried to wave him off.

"What?" Weston pressed.

Another headshake. "I just thought I remembered a swing set. But not necessarily here. Nothing about this place looks familiar."

While he wasn't sure that was true, Weston decided he wouldn't pressure her. Not now anyway.

"I'm going to try to get Daisy's DNA," he explained. "So if you notice her drinking from a cup or glass, and you get the chance to take it, do it."

"Her DNA?" Weston saw the realization flash through her eyes. "You think she could be my birth mother?"

He lifted his shoulder. "I don't know what to think at this point. I just want to rule her out. Before we left the sheriff's office, I requested a background check on her late husband."

Judging from the way the color drained from her face, she had considered the possibility that her birth mother might factor into this investigation.

"We can postpone this visit," he offered.

"No." Addie didn't hesitate, either.

Good thing, too, because when Jericho pulled

up in front of the house, the woman was in the doorway, clearly waiting for them. It was Daisy all right. She matched the photo from the DMV. Snow-white hair and with a face that showed every year of her age, but she had a sturdy build. A smile, too. But that smile did nothing to put Weston at ease.

"Don't get out yet," Weston said when Addie reached for the door handle.

Jericho confirmed that with a nod, and both the sheriff and deputy got out first. Weston followed them. All with their guns drawn. If Daisy was alarmed by that, she didn't show it. She stayed in the doorway, hugging her coat to her. A coat that could be used to conceal a weapon.

Deputy Parkman checked the left side of the house. Jericho, the right. Weston stayed put and kept an eye on Daisy and Addie.

"I got no plans to hurt anybody," Daisy volunteered.

But Weston didn't take her word for it. "Then you won't mind if I frisk you?"

"Wouldn't mind at all." She held open the coat and let him do just that. Since Daisy was almost as tall as he was, she looked him straight in the eyes while he searched her.

No weapon, and Weston didn't see one in the small living room just behind her.

"Nothing," Jericho announced, and the deputy agreed.

Only then did Weston motion for Addie to get out, and Daisy's gaze stayed on her as she made her way onto the porch.

"Come inside," Daisy offered, taking off her coat and hanging it on the hook by the door. "It's too cold to be standing out here gabbing."

It was. But since there might be hired guns inside, Weston stepped into the living room with Addie, and her brother and the deputy searched the house. It didn't take them long, just a couple of minutes, since the place wasn't that big.

"Take a seat," Daisy insisted.

Addie did, sitting on the sofa next to Daisy. The rest of them stood.

Daisy studied her. "Yep, you're that little girl that was here, all right. Faces age, they change, but eyes always stay the same."

Addie studied the woman as well, no doubt trying to figure out if she recognized her. Or if there was a family resemblance. There wasn't. Well, none that Weston could see anyway.

"You said you knew who I was," Addie prompted.

She nodded. "Me and my husband never did make money running this place so I use to do babysitting on the side. Folks came and went over the years, and one of those years, a man dropped by. Said he was a traveling salesman and that his wife had run off and that he needed somebody to watch his little girl for a week while he was looking for a new place to live. Her name was Gabrielle."

Addie repeated that name several times and then shook her head. "That doesn't sound familiar."

"The man called you Gabbie," Daisy added.

That still didn't seem to ring any bells with Addie.

"Gabbie," Daisy went on. "Didn't really fit because you said hardly more than a couple of words the whole week you were here."

"You remember the man's name?" Weston asked.

"Alton Boggs wanted to know the same thing when he came to visit. I couldn't recall it right off, but after Boggs left, I got to thinking, and I'm pretty sure the man's name was Steve Birchfield."

"I'm on it," Deputy Parkman said, taking out his phone. He stepped to the other side of the room.

Weston moved closer to Daisy. "What did this man look like?"

"Tall, lanky. Dark brown hair. Oh, and he was impatient," Daisy added after a long pause. "*Real* impatient. He didn't seem as interested in making sure his little girl was okay as he was getting out of here. Kept going on about how his wife running off was at the worst possible time and that it might cost him his job if he didn't get someone to watch the kid. The *kid*, that's what he kept calling her."

Addie looked up at Weston, and he could almost see what she was thinking. That sounded a lot like someone they'd recently met. Canales.

"Do you know Ira Canales, Boggs's campaign manager?" Weston asked.

Daisy thought about it a few seconds. "Can't say I do. He wasn't with Boggs when he came to visit a couple of months back." She paused, looked up at Weston. "Is there something creepy about Boggs, or is it just me?"

Yeah, but Weston wanted to know more about what Daisy thought. "Creepy how?"

"Well, he said he was here trying to track down anything about the little girl that the Moonlight Strangler fathered, that he was talking to lots of folks around here, but the thing is he didn't stop by any of my neighbors. Just here. I asked them, and none of them had laid eyes on him."

Interesting, and it contradicted what Boggs had told them. "So, why do you think he came to see you?"

She leaned closer as if about to tell a secret. "Well, I believe it's because he really wanted to find Steve Birchfield. That's who he was asking questions about. I figure that Birchfield fella might know something that Boggs wants to know."

"You mean like the identity of the Moonlight Strangler?" Addie asked.

Daisy shrugged. "I guess it coulda been that, but I just got the feeling that it might be, well, more."

*More* could be just Boggs's obsession with finding the person who'd murdered his childhood friend. But it could be something else. Something far more dangerous if Boggs had a more personal link to the killer.

Or if Boggs *was* the killer.

"How did Boggs know that Birchfield had been here thirty years ago?" Addie asked.

"Talk around town, I guess. Hadn't really kept it much of a secret."

Well, it hadn't been common knowledge because today was the first Weston had heard about it. Of course, there'd been plenty of leads just like this one that'd fizzled out.

"Is it possible that Steve Birchfield wasn't the little girl's father?" Weston continued.

Daisy's eyes widened. "You know, that is possible. I mean he didn't look a lick like her. And she didn't even give him so much as a goodbye when he left her here, much less a hug. When he would come by in the evenings to check on her, she'd just shy away from him."

That put a new spin on things. If Boggs turned out to be Addie's birth father, and the Moonlight Strangler, then maybe this Birchfield guy was trying to hide Addie.

"If the girl had been hurt or anything, bruises and such," Daisy went on, "I would have called somebody about that, but other than looking kinda sad and shy around her so-called daddy, she was fine the whole time she was here."

"Was there a swing set in the yard?" Addie asked.

Jericho looked surprised at the question. But not Daisy.

"Yes, there was. Honey, that was years ago. The thing rusted so bad that I had to have it hauled off to the dump. Why? You remember that?"

"No." Addie's answer was quick. "Not really. I'm probably thinking of one that used to be at the Appaloosa Pass Ranch."

A lie, but it was one Weston appreciated. Even if the swing set was a genuine memory, he didn't want her sharing it with Daisy. Not until they were certain they could trust the woman.

Deputy Parkman finished his call and walked back toward them. "There's no Steve Birchfield who matches the right age. There's also no birth record for Gabrielle or Gabbie Birchfield. You're certain that was his name?"

"That's the name he gave me," Daisy insisted.

"But I got no way of knowing if he told me the truth or not. He paid in cash, and I didn't ask for an ID or anything. It didn't work that way thirty years ago. I just trusted him to be who he said he was and didn't give it a second thought until Alton Boggs came to visit."

Yes, and Weston wanted to question Boggs further about that visit. Boggs had made it seem random, but it was looking more and more like an intentional visit. First though, Weston had another question for Daisy.

"Why didn't you call the cops when you remembered this Birchfield and the little girl?"

"I did," Daisy answered. "I called the FBI tip line number that I found in the phone book and said for them to look into it. I never heard back from them."

Probably because the FBI got hundreds of tips each day. Besides, until Addie had brought up that swing set, it really wasn't much of a connection. Forty miles was a lot of distance between here and the Crockett ranch.

"How much time was there between the little girl being dropped off here with you and Addie showing up near the Appaloosa Pass Ranch?" Jericho asked.

"I don't have any idea." Daisy's mouth trembled a little. "That was a bad time for me. My husband,

Ernest—God rest his soul—was killed in an accident. It took me a while to pull myself together."

Jericho made a sound that could have meant anything, including some sympathy. "Is that why you didn't notice Addie's picture in the papers? After my dad found her, he had the newspapers run her picture for a month or more."

Daisy shook her head. "I didn't see it, sorry. Like I said, it was a bad time for me." Her gaze went back to Addie. "Guess it was a rough time for you, too."

"I don't remember any of it," Addie assured her.

"That's probably for the best." Daisy slid her hand over Addie's. "It don't matter what name that Steve Birchfield gave me. You're the little girl that was here. I'm sure of it."

Weston had no idea if it was true, and it didn't matter. If Daisy believed it and if the Moonlight Strangler learned she might have any information about him, then Daisy might become his target.

Even though Weston didn't say that to Jericho, it was obvious it had occurred to him, too.

"Daisy, why don't you follow us into town so we can talk with the county sheriff and he can take your statement?" Jericho suggested. Except it was more of an order. "It'll be a good idea if you didn't stay here by yourself for a while. Have you got some other place you can go, like maybe to a friend or relative?"

Weston expected her to show some concern. Maybe even fear. But Daisy got to her feet and hiked up her chin. "I'm not gonna let some pea-brained serial killer run me out of my home. I'll talk to the county sheriff. I'll do all the statements you want, but when I'm done, I'm coming right back here."

Good grief. He hardly knew her, but Weston doubted she would budge on this. That meant she'd need protection. Maybe something that could be arranged with the county sheriff.

"You can ride with Daisy," Jericho told his deputy. "I'll take Weston and Addie back to Appaloosa Pass and then meet you at the county sheriff's office."

That probably meant Jericho wanted to question Daisy further. But thankfully Addie wouldn't have to be around for that. She'd already had enough put on her shoulders today. Plus, she had to be stressed about what all of this was doing to the baby.

Weston sure was.

"The FBI will need to know about this," Addie said to him on their way out the door.

They would. It was the same for Daisy. She would have to recount her story to them and probably meet with a sketch artist to come up with a composite for Birchfield. "But this might be the break we've been looking for."

A break that would only come once Addie was put through yet more tests and questions to help jog her memory. Weston only hoped she could handle anything she might recall.

After all, she could have witnessed one or more of her father's murders.

"My truck's parked by the side of the house," Daisy said to the deputy. She grabbed her cell phone, put it in her purse and locked the door behind them. "No need for you to go with me, though. I can get there all by myself."

"I'm sure you can," the deputy said, "but I was hoping you could show me the way. I'm not familiar with this area."

It was the right thing to say. Daisy clearly wanted to stand on her own two feet, but she wouldn't refuse to help someone. Or at least she wanted them to believe she was cooperating.

Weston wasn't sure which.

He took Addie's arm as they headed out the door and then remembered he didn't want anyone, including Daisy, to think they were a couple. He backed away from Addie and went ahead of the others toward the cruiser. However, he'd only made it a few steps when all hell broke loose.

And the shots rang out.

# Chapter Nine

The sounds of gunfire and Daisy's scream seemed to explode in Addie's head. The bullet had come close to her. Too close.

And before the fear and adrenaline could slam through her, Weston had his arm around her and dragged her to the ground on the side of the concrete steps that led up to the porch.

Not a second too soon.

Because another shot came her way and smashed into the dirt where she'd just been standing.

She was definitely the target, and the shots seemed to be coming from the old barn out in what was left of the pasture. There was another gunman. One who clearly wanted her dead.

Deputy Mack Parkman was on the porch, and he took hold of a still-screaming Daisy and pushed her behind some rocking chairs. Jericho took up cover behind the step railing. They were all out in the open.

All vulnerable.

Again.

Addie cursed the fact that once again her blood ties had put people in danger. Including her baby.

When was this going to stop?

At least Weston and she were semiprotected by the steps, but the railing and the rocking chairs weren't nearly enough to stop bullets. Mack and Daisy were especially vulnerable, but the shooter didn't take aim at them.

She hoped that wasn't because the shooter and Daisy were working together. But if they were, Daisy was putting up a good act because the woman seemed genuinely terrified.

Addie sure was.

The fear rose in her throat. Bitter and cold like the air. She had to fight to hold on to her breath, had to fight to keep it steady, too. It wouldn't do anyone any good if she hyperventilated or panicked.

More shots came, one right behind the other. Weston stayed down on the ground with her, sheltering her with his body. Jericho, however, lifted his head and gun, and he fired in the direction of the barn.

"You see him?" Weston asked.

Jericho shook his head. "Not yet. One of us needs to get into the cruiser and pull it closer."

Since it was bullet resistant, that's exactly

where she wanted to be, but she wanted the others in there, too. However, the cruiser was a good fifteen feet away, and there was nothing but open space between it and the porch.

"Stay down," Weston told her.

But Weston didn't stay down. "Cover me," he told Jericho a split second before he moved off her. Only then did Addie realize he was heading for the cruiser.

Almost immediately, their attacker sent some shots Weston's way. Addie's heart pounded even harder, her throat tightened, and she could only watch, and pray, as Weston scrambled across the ground.

Jericho fired at the barn, and with the shots coming from the gunman, the sound was almost deafening. It seemed to take Weston an eternity to dive to the side of the cruiser, but she figured it was mere seconds.

"Keys," Jericho said, and he tossed them to Weston.

Weston didn't waste any time opening the cruiser door closest to him, and he climbed in. Started the engine.

The gunman was fixed on Weston now. Or rather on the cruiser tires. Addie had no idea if they, too, were bullet or puncture resistant. If they weren't and if the gunman managed to shoot them out, they'd be stuck. Yes, Daisy's truck was on the side of the house, but it would be dangerous to try to get to it.

Of course, staying put would be dangerous, as well.

One of the bullets slammed into the front tire, but that didn't stop Weston from driving forward. He maneuvered the cruiser so that the passenger's side door was aligned with the steps and so that the cruiser was literally blocking the path of the gunman's shots.

Weston threw open the passenger's side door for her. "Get in."

Addie moved as fast as she could, scurrying across the seat toward Weston. The gunman adjusted his shots, trying to shoot out the window. The glass webbed but thankfully held.

Weston threw the cruiser into reverse, backed up and maneuvered it again so that it was closer to Jericho. More shots came, some of them slicing across the porch. Her brother hurried down the steps and jumped into the front seat with them.

"I'll move into position so that Daisy and Mack can get in the backseat," Weston said.

And he had already started to do that when the shots stopped. They didn't just trail off, either. They stopped completely. It didn't take Addie long to figure out why. She saw the man running from the back of the barn.

"Hell, no," Weston grumbled. "He's not getting away. Stay with Addie," he added to Jericho.

Addie reached for him, but she wasn't nearly as fast as Weston was. He bolted from the cruiser and took off after the gunman.

It was a footrace now, and the shooter had a big head start on Weston. Plus, at any moment the man could turn around and fire. There weren't a lot of places that Weston could use for cover. Of course, Weston could fire, too, but they needed this man alive so he could tell them what the heck was going on.

"Go help Weston," she said to Jericho.

Her brother shook his head. "This could be a trap. There could be another gunman out here, waiting to get you alone."

Oh, God. She hadn't even considered that, but it was true. This was the second attempt to kill her, and it was obvious that whoever was behind this would do pretty much anything to make sure she was dead.

But why?

Addie kept going back to the initial threat from the Moonlight Strangler. He'd been afraid that she might remember something.

And maybe she had.

That swing set was becoming clearer and clearer in her mind. Did that mean she'd really been here all those years ago? Addie figured soon, very soon, she'd give that more thought, but for now she just watched Weston and prayed that they all got out of this alive.

Jericho kept watch, too, his gaze firing all around them. Mack did, as well. Daisy was no longer screaming, but she was sobbing and begging Mack to get her to the hospital.

That's when Addie spotted the blood on the woman's arm.

"I think Daisy's been shot," Addie let Jericho know.

Her brother cursed when he glanced up at the porch. "How bad is she hurt?" he called out to Mack.

Mack shook his head. "She was cut by some wood flying up off the porch. She'll need stitches."

That didn't sound life-threatening, thank goodness, but Daisy had to be terrified. Addie certainly was.

Unlike Weston.

He was charging forward, fast, closing the distance between him and the gunman.

"Watch out!" she shouted to Weston when she saw the man bring up his gun.

He fired.

But so did Weston.

And the gunman crumpled to the ground.

NORMALLY A DEAD hit man wouldn't give Weston a moment's pause, but he'd needed this one alive. Too bad Weston had been forced to kill or be killed.

"Maybe Jericho will find something when he checks the hit man's body," Addie said. "A phone. More photos. Something to tell us why he came after me again today."

Her words were right. Hopeful, even. However, Weston didn't see any of that hope in her eyes or body language. Of course, the adrenaline crash might have something to do with that. She looked past just being plain tired.

And probably was.

In addition to surviving two attacks, she was dealing with all the other stuff. The baby. The memories that might be returning.

Him.

All of that was taking a toll.

"I want you to get some rest," Weston insisted the moment they stepped into the ranch house. Her brother Jax had already searched it, and two armed ranch hands were standing guard at both the front and the back of the house. The alarm system was on, too.

Security was in place.

Now to make sure Addie didn't go into overload. She was already blinking back tears, and any little thing could push her over the edge.

His phone dinged, and while trying to brace himself for more bad news, Weston looked down at the screen. Nothing bad. Everything considered, it was actually good news.

"Your mom's settled at her sister's house, and Jericho hired a private bodyguard to stay with them," Weston said, reading the text. "And Jericho managed to get a DNA sample from Daisy."

"She volunteered it?"

"Not exactly. She refused when Jericho asked, but her blood was on Mack's shirt so we got it anyway."

"Oh." The disappointment was there now. "I didn't expect her to refuse. I thought maybe she'd want to help in any way possible."

Not judging from the woman's reaction when they'd gotten her to the hospital. She'd barely spoken a word to them, but Weston had heard her tell the doctor that she didn't want any of the Crocketts or Weston near her.

He couldn't blame Daisy if she was truly innocent in all of this, but the jury was still out on that, and he always found it suspicious when a suspect refused a DNA request. It usually meant they were hiding something. Of course, she could have merely been reacting to the ordeal she'd just been through.

Weston slipped his arm around her waist to lead her to the sofa in the adjoining living room. He figured he stood a better chance of getting her to take a nap there than he did taking her upstairs.

Besides, it would be a really bad idea for him to try to put her to bed.

Addie's defenses were down. His, too. Added to the crash of emotions, and a bed would feel more like a powder keg. That's the reason Weston let go of her as soon as he had her seated. But Addie fixed that. She took his hand and pulled him down next to her.

"What if Daisy's a match?" Addie wasn't talking to him exactly but more to herself. "What if she's my birth mother?"

"Then, it'll soon put an end to this. Because if she is, she'll tell us the identity of your birth father, and we can arrest him."

Weston was certain of that. If Daisy knew who the Moonlight Strangler was, then he'd make sure she talked. Along with paying for anything that she'd done wrong. Including abandoning her child.

"Good. Maybe she'll be a match." Addie's breath was weary now. Like the rest of her. "I want to get on with my life. I want normal again."

"Good luck with that," Weston said before actually thinking about what he was saying. "I meant the pregnancy, the baby. That'll change things."

Not just for them but for her entire family.

She nodded. "Mom's already planning on turning one of the guest rooms into a nursery."

Of course she would want to raise the baby here. Her home. A place where three generations of Crocketts had been raised.

But it wasn't Weston's home.

And even though Jericho and he had worked out a somewhat shaky peace agreement for the sake of the investigation, Weston doubted any of the Crockett lawmen would ever welcome him there.

His phone dinged again. Instant tightening in his chest, and it tightened even more when he read through the lengthy text.

"Bad news?" Addie asked.

"Ogden is being transferred to the hospital at the jail. His lawyer is going to use an insanity defense to try to get him moved to a mental facility."

She touched his forehead. "That didn't put the worry lines there. What else happened?"

"The safe house is ready."

Addie studied him. "How soon do I leave?"

"Soon. The marshals will be here in an hour or so."

"That is soon," she said under her breath. Then, the realization flashed through her eyes. "You won't be going with me?"

Weston decided to make this as light as possible. "No. Sounds like you'll miss me, though."

It was a dumber-than-dirt thing to say. She probably wouldn't miss him, but there were still those little flashes of fire between them, and that was creating this pull inside him. Maybe inside her, too.

*Definitely* inside her, he decided, when their eyes met.

Those little flashes of fire were starting up again.

"I don't want to be attracted to you," she insisted.

That wasn't much of a surprise. But it was a surprise when her mouth suddenly came to his.

Everything inside him yelled that this was a mistake. It complicated an already complicated situation.

Did that stop him?

No.

In fact, Weston pushed his dumber-than-dirt actions to the limit. He slipped his hand around the back of her neck, pulled her to him and kissed her the way he'd been wanting to kiss her for months now. He figured if he was going to make a mistake, then it might as well be a good one.

And this one was *good.*

Yeah, that taste always got to him. The feel of her in his arms, too. It was obviously getting to Addie as well because she wiggled closer and closer until they were plastered against each other.

Great.

Now they weren't just kissing, they had advanced to a full-blown make-out session. While being alone in the house. And those little flashes of fire snapped high and hot when her hand landed on his chest.

She stopped, looked up at him, and a shivery breath left her mouth. *Finally.* She had come to her senses and was finally putting a stop to something they should have never started.

But no.

She pulled him back to her as if starved for him. Weston knew the feeling, and he also knew that kisses and touches were only going to skyrocket that need.

And they did.

He was clearly brainless when it came to Addie, and he proved it by lowering the kisses to her throat. She'd been his lover. For three whole days. Enough time for him to have learned how to pleasure her. Too bad she'd learned the same about him, because while Weston was kissing the tops of her breasts, she put her hand on his stomach.

Oh, man.

He was in big trouble here, and while sleeping with her again would please every inch of his body, it would also distract him at the worst possible time.

Weston got instant proof of that when he heard one of the ranch hands shout his name.

Weston cursed himself, and he practically jumped off the sofa while drawing his gun. "Stay away from the windows," he warned Addie, and he rushed to the door.

"We got a visitor," the ranch hand called out to him. "A truck's coming up the road right now."

Well, at least it wasn't someone climbing over

the fence. And it could be the marshals arriving a little earlier than planned. Weston disarmed the security system so he could open the door and stepped onto the porch.

The ranch hands and Weston all trained their guns on the truck as it pulled to a stop in front of the house. The windows were heavily tinted so Weston didn't get a look at their visitor until he threw open the truck door.

Definitely a stranger.

Tall, lanky with sandy brown hair. Jeans, cowboy boots and a Stetson hat. He looked like a cowboy. Until he flashed a badge when he stepped from the truck.

"I'm Special Agent Cord Granger, DEA," he said.

DEA? Not a marshal. He handed his badge to one of the ranch hands. "It looks real," the hand relayed to Weston.

"It *is* real," the man assured them. Not exactly a friendly sort, but then Weston wasn't in a friendly mood, either.

"Stay right there until I verify who you are," Weston insisted. "We've had some trouble lately."

"Yeah," Granger grumbled, but didn't come closer.

Without taking his eyes off the man, Weston called Jericho. "A DEA agent just showed up here. Cord Granger. Can you make sure this isn't another hit man?"

Jericho didn't say a word, but, as he'd done when Addie had asked him to verify Weston's identity, he got straight to work. "He's DEA. Records sealed. I'm texting you his photo."

Weston waited for the picture to load. Yes, it was Granger all right.

"I'll call you back after I find out why he's here," Weston said to Jericho, and he ended the call.

"I'm Weston Cade, Texas Ranger." And now that they'd gotten introductions out of the way, Weston went for the obvious. "What do you want?"

"To speak to Addie Crockett."

Now, why would a DEA agent want to see her? Unless her birth father was on the DEA's radar. If so, she wasn't exactly up to a round of questioning.

"Is this about the Moonlight Strangler?" Weston demanded.

He didn't jump to answer that, but finally mumbled another "Yeah."

Weston heard the movement behind him and cursed when he realized Addie hadn't stayed put.

"What about the Moonlight Strangler?" she asked.

Again, the agent didn't jump to answer. But

his gaze fixed on Addie as he made his way toward them.

Weston glanced at her and saw that her attention was on the visitor, as well. "You know this guy?"

"No," Addie and the agent answered in unison.

He stepped onto the porch with them. Addie and the agent continued staring at each other.

"I don't remember you," Granger said almost in a whisper. "I thought, *hoped*, maybe I would."

"Who the hell are you?" Weston snapped.

It took Granger several more moments to look away from Addie. Then he extended his hand for Weston to shake. "The Moonlight Strangler is my biological father. I'm Addie's brother."

# *Chapter Ten*

Addie's head was still spinning from the spent adrenaline and the kissing session with Weston. Spinning so much that she was certain she'd misunderstood what this DEA agent had just said.

"Her brother?" Weston challenged.

She was glad Weston had asked because it took Addie a moment to find her voice. "How?" Considering there was a whirlwind in her head, Addie was glad she could come up with a question.

Now she needed an answer.

One that Cord Granger didn't jump to give her. Instead, he glanced around. A lawman's glance, one that showed he was uneasy. And Addie didn't think that unease was all because of this bombshell of a meeting.

"We need to talk," he finally said to her. "And I'd rather not hang around on the porch with you standing there. Especially after what happened earlier."

Addie saw the fierce debate in Weston's eyes

before he finally stepped back so that Cord could enter. Weston shut the door, but he kept himself between her and their visitor.

"Start talking," Weston told him. "And what you say had better make sense, or I'm tossing you out of here."

"None of this makes sense," Cord said. But then he huffed and put his hands on his hips, his gaze going to her, not Weston. "I compared my DNA to the Moonlight Strangler, and it was a match. A match to yours, too, Addie. We're fraternal twins."

A twin brother. *Her* brother. Addie had never lacked for siblings since she already had four brothers, but it'd been years since she'd considered the possibility of a biological one. "Why didn't you come forward sooner?" Weston snapped. "Addie's known for three months about the DNA match."

Cord shook his head. "I was on a deep cover assignment. No way for anyone to contact me. And because of what I do, my DNA isn't in the normal law enforcement databases so that's why there wasn't an immediate hit."

She looked at Weston to see if that was standard, and he nodded. He still didn't seem as if he was buying this, though.

"After I got off assignment," Cord continued, "I learned about Addie's DNA match, read about her background. It was too similar to mine so I had my DNA compared to hers and the Moonlight Strangler."

"Your background?" she questioned.

"When I was three, I was abandoned in the men's room of a gas station about a hundred miles from Appaloosa Pass. It was the same day you showed up here at the Crockett ranch. I don't have any memories of those things, but I learned about both later."

Cord's gaze slid around the foyer. Not exactly elegant, but Addie knew her family had a lot more than most. "You were lucky," he added.

Addie got the feeling that it hadn't been the same for him. She also got the feeling that it was something he didn't want to discuss with her. Not with anybody.

Almost frantically, she studied Cord's face and saw some features that were like hers. The eyes, mainly. And his mouth. Yes, a definite resemblance even though his hair was a lot darker than hers.

She didn't want to take a leap of faith and believe this man. But she did. There was something, maybe genetic memories or the weird bond between twins, but she knew in her heart that this was indeed her brother.

Weston's scowl, however, told her he didn't feel the same. "I want proof of what you're saying," he insisted.

"I figured you would. You have a reputation for being…driven. I had the DNA results couriered to Sheriff Crockett." He checked his watch. "He should have them by now."

While keeping himself in front of Addie, Weston took out his phone and called Jericho. He put it on speaker when Jericho answered, and he opened his mouth, no doubt ready to tell her brother what was going on, but Jericho beat him to it.

"I just got a classified DNA report on some federal agent. A Joe. What the hell do you know about this?"

"A Joe?" she questioned.

"Slang for deep cover," Weston explained. "What's in the report?" he asked Jericho.

Cord's gaze met hers while they waited, and Addie could have sworn a dozen things passed between them.

Memories, maybe?

Not of the swing set this time, but a toy. A stuffed brown bear. And a little boy handing it to her. It came like a flash and was gone before she could even try to hang on to it.

"According to this, Addie has a biological brother," Jericho snapped.

"Yeah, and the *brother* is here at the ranch," Weston supplied.

Jericho cursed. "And you let him in?"

"It's okay," Addie spoke up.

"Hell, no, it's not okay," Jericho fired back. "He might be a DEA agent, but we don't know if we can trust him."

"I trust him," she said. That earned her a scowl from Weston and more profanity from Jericho.

"I'm on my way out there," Jericho insisted, and he ended the call.

If Cord had a reaction to that, he didn't show it. In fact, he showed no emotion at all when his attention went back to Weston. "Why would I lie about this?"

"Because you could be a serial killer groupie, someone who wants to get close to Addie."

Cord held the stare between them. "It appears she already has enough people close to her."

Addie couldn't help it. She smiled, though heaven knew there was nothing to smile about.

"Do you remember anything about me?" Addie asked him. "About your childhood?"

"No." Unlike his other responses, it was fast. "When I found out about the DNA match, I went through hypnosis, therapy and lots of questioning. *Lots.* No memories before age four, but my handler pulled me from duty until they could get all of this sorted out."

That tightened his jaw.

She'd known this man only a few minutes, but Addie knew that had cut him to the core.

"The DEA is working on the case?" Weston asked.

"Plenty of people are working on it. Me included. Until the Moonlight Strangler is caught, killed or otherwise put out of circulation, the Justice Department believes I shouldn't be in the field doing a job that I'm damn good at."

Yes, a cut to the core.

"So that's why you came here?" Addie asked. "You want to help us find him and vice versa so you can get back to work?"

He paused again. A long time. Then nodded. "And I wanted to meet you, to see if it spurred something."

She knew exactly how he felt.

"And?" Weston pressed.

"Nothing." Another pause. Cord's mouth tightened as if he'd tasted something bitter. "But there is some kind of connection. One I don't particularly want to feel because I don't want to worry about your safety. Is she safe?" he asked Weston.

"She soon will be."

Addie hoped that was true. Hoped it was true for her *brother*. But she doubted Cord would be going to a safe house. No. He wasn't the safe house type.

"What have you learned about the Moonlight Strangler?" Weston asked.

"I don't have a name. I'm guessing you don't, either, or there would have been an arrest. I just have a list of suspects, too many questions and nowhere near enough answers."

That got her attention. Weston's, too. "I want that list of suspects," Weston insisted.

Cord nodded. "And I want yours. Is Daisy Vogel on it?"

"Yeah," Weston confirmed. "Soon, I want to have a chat with her. What do you know about her?"

"Not as much as I want to know. She wasn't on my radar until the attack today. I've been monitoring what you've been doing, and when I saw you make the trip to her place, I ran a background check on her."

Weston took a step closer and got right in his face. "Did you know the attack was going to happen?"

"Of course not. I have no motive for you or Addie to be hurt. Or worse." He reached out, touched the scar on her cheek. "In fact, there's every reason for her to stay alive so we can catch this killer. What do you remember?" he asked her without even pausing for a breath.

For so long Addie's response had been nothing. And it'd been true. Until today. "A swing set. I think it was at Daisy's house, and she admitted that thirty years ago she babysat a little girl who might have been me."

"But I wasn't with you?"

She shook her head. "A man named Steve Birchfield took me to her and left me there for a week. Is he on your suspect list?"

"He is now." Cord took out his phone, fired off a quick text. "I'll see if there's anything on him."

"Jericho and I are already doing that," Weston snarled.

"Good. I'll take anything I can get." Cord's gaze shifted back to her. "You remember anything else?"

"I don't know. Everything's muddled, and I'm not sure if it's an actual memory from those days or something that happened after I arrived here at the ranch."

"Did you remember something?" Weston asked her. No snarling tone now, but he took her by the shoulders. "This is too much for you."

Addie had been about to assure him that she could handle it, but the truth was, her head was spinning, and she suddenly felt queasy. But not just queasy—she was about to throw up. She hadn't experienced any morning sickness yet, but she thought she might be getting a full dose of it now.

"Excuse me a minute." She didn't wait for

Weston to agree. She hurried toward the powder room just up in the hall, and she got there in the nick of time.

Good grief.

She didn't need this now with everything else going on, but there was never a good time for morning sickness. As icky as it was, at least it was a reminder of the pregnancy. Of the baby. A reminder, too, that she needed to take better care of herself.

Weston and Cord must have agreed with that since they were both waiting for her in the hall when she opened the door.

"I'm not going to ask you if you're all right," Weston said, scooping her up in his arms, "because clearly you're not. I'm calling the doctor."

"Don't, please. I just need a cracker or something. There's some in the pantry in the kitchen."

Weston eased her onto the sofa, turned as if to go get the crackers, but then he no doubt remembered that would mean leaving her alone with Cord, a man he didn't trust.

"I'll get them," Cord volunteered, and he headed out of the room.

"How are you—really?" Weston asked her when they were alone.

Addie tried to give him a reassuring look. Failed miserably. Hard to look reassuring with her stomach lurching. "All the pregnancy books say this is normal."

"How long will it last?"

Addie lifted her hands. "A few months. Maybe longer. Some women have it the entire pregnancy."

He cursed and looked as if he wanted to continue the cursing for a long time. "I'm so sorry."

She managed another smile and took his hand. "I'll live." Except that was a reminder she might not if they didn't stop the Moonlight Strangler.

Weston tipped his head toward the kitchen and sat down next to her. "Do you believe him?"

"Yes," Addie said without hesitation.

A muscle flickered in his jaw. "Did you sense you had a biological brother?"

"No. Well, I used to think about it when I was a kid, but I wasn't really lacking in the brother and family department." Unlike Cord. "I guess those thoughts of sibling possibilities got overshadowed by the real ones."

"And what about the memories?" he asked.

But she didn't get a chance to answer because Cord came back in with a box of crackers and a glass of water. He set them on the coffee table in front of her.

"How far along are you in the pregnancy?" Cord asked. Obviously, he'd put two and two together.

"Three months." She took out a cracker, nibbled on it. Hoped it would help.

Cord glanced at their ring fingers. No rings, but since she still had hold of Weston's hands, Cord no doubt figured out the answer to a question he probably wouldn't have asked anyway—who was the baby's father?

The next look he gave Weston was more of a glare. One she recognized.

Mercy.

She didn't need another brother fighting her battles for her.

"Memories," she reminded both of them. That got their attention back on track. "I might have one. A stuffed bear. You handing it to me."

Cord took a deep breath, and he sank down into the chair across from them. He closed his eyes a moment as if to force that memory to the surface. "Were there Christmas lights?"

She hadn't remembered that. Only the little boy with the brown hair and eyes that were the same color as hers.

Like Cord's.

Addie closed her eyes as well, hoping for some other fragment of the memory. But nothing.

"We can both go back through hypnosis," Cord suggested. "In the meantime, we need to do something to draw out the killer."

"You're not using her as bait," Weston snapped.

Cord's gaze went to her stomach. "No. Not now, I won't. But I could be bait. I figure if he learns

I'm remembering things, then he'll want me dead. He doesn't have to know that the memories are of Christmas lights and a brown stuffed bear."

Addie pulled back her shoulders. "I didn't mention the color of the bear."

Cord paused, nodded. "Yeah, we definitely need to be hypnotized again."

Weston didn't argue with that. "Who's on your suspect list?" he asked Cord.

"Alton Boggs," he readily answered. "I'm sure you've reached the same conclusion, that he's way too interested in the Moonlight Strangler for this not to be personal."

"Agreed," Weston said. "What about Canales?"

"He's on the list, too. Maybe one or both are the Moonlight Strangler."

That didn't help her queasy stomach. "You think they're killing together?"

"Could be. I found a criminal informant who said that Boggs and Canales used to be involved in a gunrunning operation. There's nothing about it in any of their background checks," Cord added when Weston reached for his phone. "But the CI claims it was going on thirty years ago."

Weston stayed quiet a moment. "Did the CI think the murders were tied to the gunrunning?"

"The initial ones, yes. Then, he thought maybe the killer or killers got a taste for it."

It sickened her to think of it, but this could be the link they'd been searching for.

"I want the name of this CI," Weston insisted.

"She's dead." Cord glanced away from them. "I'm pretty sure I got her killed. I didn't think the Moonlight Strangler was watching me, but I was wrong. The SOB cut her on the cheek. Left his mark to make sure I'd see it."

"I'm sorry," Weston told him. Considering what her birth father had done to Collette, Addie was sure it was a sincere apology.

It didn't take Cord long to regain his composure. "I haven't had any luck connecting the first victims to either Canales or Boggs. Or to the Moonlight Strangler for that matter."

"I tried to get a DNA sample from Boggs. He didn't go for it," Weston said. "But we should have Canales's results back in a day or two. I told the lab to put a rush on it. We're also running DNA on the man who tried to kill Addie. Lonny Ogden. He's too young to be the Moonlight Strangler, but I want to make sure he's not connected to one of the victims."

"I'll see what I can do about getting DNA from Boggs." Cord opened his mouth to say more, but a sound stopped him.

A car approaching the house.

Weston hurried to the window and looked out. "It's Jericho."

The relief came—this wasn't the start of another attack. But the relief went just as fast. Addie stood to try to brace herself for what would no doubt turn into a testosterone contest, but when her brother came through the door, he wasn't focused on Cord. He was on the phone and was cursing at the person on the other end of the line.

"Find her," Jericho snapped, and at the same moment he ended the call, he aimed an expected glare at Cord. "You'd damn well better not be here to hurt Addie because I don't have time to deal with you."

"What's wrong?" Weston asked Jericho.

"Daisy's missing."

That got Addie on her feet. "What happened?"

Jericho had to get his teeth unclenched before he could speak. "I don't know yet, but I'm pretty sure her disappearance has something to do with *this*. It was left on the answering machine at Daisy's house, and I got the county deputy to play it for me."

Her brother lifted his phone and hit the play button on the recording.

# Chapter Eleven

"Daisy, you need to disappear. *Fast.* Staying around here won't be good for your health. Leave and take this phone and answering machine with you."

Weston heard the message Jericho had just played for them, and he didn't know whether to groan or curse. So, he did both.

"That's Lonny Ogden's voice," Addie said.

Yes, it was. Weston had only heard the man speak a couple of times, but he was sure of it. What was that idiot up to now?

"First of all, how did Ogden get access to a phone?" Weston asked Jericho. "And how the heck does he know Daisy?"

"I don't have the answer to either of those things, but I'm about to find out." He made another call. "Jax," Jericho said when his brother answered, "set up a video chat with the dirtbag who left that threatening message for Daisy. Call me when you've got him on the line."

Jericho hit the end-call as his gaze snapped to Cord. "If you're here to try to talk Addie into doing something stupid, dangerous or otherwise, then there's the door." He hitched is thumb in that direction.

"I'm here to find a killer," Cord said, meeting him head-on.

Jericho tapped his badge. "Newsflash. We're all here for that, but you're not using my sister as bait."

Weston stepped to Jericho's side—despite the glare Jericho gave Weston to remind him that he'd wanted to do the same thing. Finally, here was something Jericho and he could agree on.

"I don't want Addie in danger, either," Cord said. He was probably telling the truth.

*Probably.*

However, Weston knew that kind of drive, that kind of hunger for justice, and a hunger like that just might override any feelings Cord had for a twin sister he hardly knew.

"I'm standing right here," Addie reminded them. "Last I checked, I could speak for myself."

"You aren't going to do or *say* anything to put yourself in further danger," Jericho argued.

Probably because Jericho looked ready to implode, she leaned in and kissed him on the cheek. "I won't be safe until the Moonlight Strangler is caught. Cord and I might have some new memories that could help."

"Fragments of memories," Weston corrected when Jericho stared at them.

A bear and a swing set. Childhood things that could have a huge impact if they were true and could be connected to other memories.

Too bad memories like that could make Addie even more of a target than she already was.

"I was about to call the FBI," Weston added. "I want them to go to the safe house and do the hypnosis once Addie's there."

Which shouldn't be long at all since the marshals were probably on their way. Of course, he'd gotten distracted from making that call because he'd been kissing Addie. Then Cord had arrived.

"So, that DEA agent's really your brother?" Jericho asked her.

She nodded. "I think so, yes."

Weston wasn't exactly sure what he saw in Jericho's eyes. Frustration.

Maybe a little jealousy.

He clearly loved Addie and had been a good brother to her all these years. But blood was blood. Or at least Jericho might see it that way. However, Weston figured blood would never come between the love Addie had for Jericho and the rest of her adoptive family.

Cord's phone buzzed at the same moment as

Jericho's, and Cord stepped into the foyer once he saw the name of the caller on the screen. Weston kept an eye on him, but the bulk of his attention went to Jericho's phone. It was Jax, and he'd obviously managed to set up a video call. Judging from the background, he was at the hospital.

"Jax, put a camera on that weasel so I can see his face when he's talking to me," Jericho instructed. "If he lies, punch him."

Jax flexed his eyebrows in a *sure-whatever* gesture and turned the phone so they could see Ogden's face.

"Start talking," Jericho ordered the man. "Why'd you leave that message for Daisy Vogel?"

Ogden's eyes widened. "Because she didn't answer when I called her."

Weston moved in front of the phone screen so that Ogden could see his glare. "That's not helping your case. Why leave that message?"

"Because I had to."

That was it, apparently the only explanation Ogden intended to give them. Well, it wasn't enough.

"If you don't want to hurt more than you're hurting right now," Weston warned him, "then start talking."

Ogden glanced around the room as if looking for some kind of help, but since only Jax was there, he must have decided that he was on his own. "August McCain forced me to make the call. He even wrote down what I was to say."

Addie shook her head. "Who's August McCain?"

"His lawyer," Jericho growled. "Where is he?"

"He left. And he said he wouldn't be coming back. He also said I was to keep my mouth shut."

Jericho cursed, handed Weston his phone before he stepped away to use the land line in the foyer. "I'll get someone out looking for him. See what else you can get from this piece of work."

Gladly. "Why did McCain want you to scare Daisy, and did he do anything to her?"

"Do anything? Oh, man. You don't think he'd hurt her?"

"I don't know. You tell me."

Ogden frantically shook his head. "It was just supposed to be words. No violence. And it wasn't my idea. I was just the messenger."

Maybe. "Convince me of that."

Ogden no doubt heard that for the threat it was. He swallowed hard. "I've got no beef with Daisy. Heck, I don't even know her. Check my phone records. Today was the first time I'd ever called her."

Weston would indeed check those phone records. "Why'd McCain want her out of the picture?"

No eye widening this time, but Weston did see

something he recognized. Ogden knew the answer to the question. "I can't tell you anything else." He leaned in closer to the phone screen. "McCain's dangerous."

"And you don't think I am? I'm the one who shot you. There's a pecking order for dangerous, and I'm at the top of it. Now talk!"

Ogden did more of that glancing around until his attention came back to Weston. Weston made sure he was all lawman now. A lawman who'd do pretty much whatever it took to get to the truth. After all, Addie and the baby's safety were at stake here.

"I don't know all the details," Ogden finally said, "but it has something to do with a gunrunning mess. Not recent stuff but something that happened a real long time ago. Like maybe before I was even born."

Was it the same operation that might have involved Boggs and Canales? As much as Weston wanted to know, it wasn't a good idea to share that info with the likes of Ogden.

"Keep talking," Weston insisted.

"I don't know much more other than Daisy's husband might have been involved in it. I think that's what I heard McCain say anyway."

Since Cord had finished his call, Weston motioned for him to start checking on the woman's late husband. "Ernest Vogel," he mouthed to Cord.

Weston turned his attention back to Ogden. "Did this gunrunning have something to do with the Moonlight Strangler?" he asked.

Addie moved closer, no doubt wanting to hear the answer. Maybe dreading it, too, since Weston could see the pulse throbbing on her throat.

"I think so," Ogden finally said. "But I'm not sure what exactly. That's the truth," he quickly added when Weston scowled. "I think maybe all of this has something to do with the first victim."

"Leta Dooley," Addie provided.

Even though Cord was on the phone in the other room, he obviously heard her and nodded. He also repeated the woman's name to the person he'd called.

Apparently, both Cord and Addie knew the list of victims as well as Weston. Leta was the first *known* victim anyway. The Moonlight Strangler's signature wasn't to hide bodies, but it was possible he'd done that early on when he'd started his killing spree. If so, there was no telling how many victims there were.

"You got what you need from Ogden?" Jax asked. "The jail guards are here to move him."

Weston nodded. "I got what I need *for now*. But, Ogden, if any of this is a lie, I'll be making a personal visit to the jail."

Weston ended the call and turned to Jericho.

Both Cord and he were still on their phones while Addie volleyed attention among all three of them.

"Daisy has to be okay," she whispered.

Hell. Addie was shaky again. Looked ready for another round of morning sickness, too, so Weston had her sit back down on the sofa.

"It's possible Daisy was involved in the gun-running operation," Weston reminded her.

Or involved with the murders.

Weston kept that to himself since Addie was already pale enough. Best not to remind her that her former babysitter could have been an accessory to murder. Or even more.

"My brother Chase is a marshal, but Jericho said Chase was tied up on an assignment and can't get here in time to go to the safe house. Will you go with me?" she asked.

That wasn't a question Weston expected to hear. He'd been sure Addie wanted to put some distance between them. Especially since distance seemed to be the only thing that would prevent his mouth from locating hers again for more of those mind-clouding kisses.

"For the marshals, I'll be just a job to them," she added, and she slid her hand over her stomach.

Yeah, she would be. But not for Weston. "I'll go with you."

And somehow figure out how to run his part of the investigation from the safe house.

He hadn't intended to do it, but he slipped his arm around her and pulled her closer. Along with brushing a kiss on her forehead. It didn't help. Well, didn't help with that jittery look in her eyes, and it earned him a really nasty glare from Jericho.

Then one from Cord.

Weston didn't budge, not even when the pair finished their calls and came toward them.

Jericho finally dropped the glare and cursed before he started talking. "According to his office, McCain's on a leave of absence. Family emergency that just popped up, his assistant said. I just put out a BOLO on him. On Daisy, too. The county sheriff is on the way to her house to see if she's gone back there."

Weston doubted she had. If Daisy was innocent, she was no doubt afraid for her life, especially since she'd already been injured in the latest attack. And if she was guilty, then she wouldn't want lawmen to find her, and her house was the first place they'd look.

"Did you freeze her bank accounts?" Weston asked.

Jericho nodded. "I'm trying to do the same to McCain, but it's a little trickier with him. He's well-connected, and he's trying to use those connections to stonewall us. It won't work. We'll find him."

Weston hoped that was true, but McCain had a head start on them, and the lawyer could use those very connections and his resources to disappear.

Cord finally finished his call, and he made his way back toward them, as well. "Daisy's husband, Ernest, died in a tractor accident on or very near the same day Addie and I were abandoned."

That fit with what Daisy had told them.

"The coroner originally listed it as a suspicious death but then changed it to an accident," Cord explained. "The coroner was Alton Boggs's uncle."

Hell. That wasn't a good connection. Well, except that it might make it easier to get Boggs's DNA now if they could prove Boggs conspired with his uncle to cover up a crime.

"I've got my sources working on finding a link between the gunrunning, Daisy, her husband, Boggs and Canales," Cord added. "But the coroner died years ago, and his notes were destroyed in an office fire."

Convenient. But more likely a cover-up.

"I'll get my sources working on it, too," Jericho insisted. "I also want to find out who the heck Steve Birchfield is and if that was an alias. It could have been Boggs or Canales using that name."

Cord only nodded, and he glanced at the notes he'd made. "The first victim, Leta Dooley, lived about ten miles from Daisy, and her body was found three days after Ernest's tractor *accident*.

She had a record for prostitution, and at the time of her murder, she was living with a lowlife who beat her on a regular basis. A few years later, he was arrested for—you probably guessed it—gunrunning."

Bingo. They were coming full circle now, all the players in place at the time of the gunrunning operation and the start of the murders. Maybe Leta had learned the wrong thing about the wrong person.

Like Boggs.

"Is Leta's old *heartthrob* still alive?" Jericho asked, the sarcasm dripping from the term of endearment.

Cord shook his head. "Dead, too. Car accident. And yes, the same coroner signed off on it."

And that meant Boggs had some explaining to do about this uncle.

"There's more," Cord went on. "Leta had a son. The kid disappeared into the foster care system after she was murdered, but I've set tracers on him. He might know something about what really happened to his mom."

Weston hoped all of this would lead to something.

The sound of a car engine had Weston, Jericho and Cord all drawing their weapons, but when Weston hurried to the window, he holstered his. That's because he recognized the marshal who stepped from the car. It was Daniel Seaver, and he and his partner were there to take Addie, and him, to the safe house.

Jericho headed to the front door to let them in.

"You should get your things ready to go," Weston told Addie.

She nodded. "My bag's upstairs, but I'd like to freshen up before I leave."

Since Addie still didn't look too steady on her feet, Weston took her arm to help her navigate the steps. However, they didn't make it far before Jericho's phone buzzed. He put it on speaker, and Weston stopped when he heard Jax's frantic voice from the other end of the line.

"Bad news," Jax said. "You need to shut down the ranch now. Lonny Ogden just escaped."

# *Chapter Twelve*

Addie figured she should feel panic over Ogden's escape, but maybe she was past that point. This seemed like just another setback in a string of setbacks.

"How did this happen?" she asked at the same moment Weston and Jericho voiced a similar version of the question. Hers, though, wasn't laced with profanity like theirs.

"I'm not sure," Jax answered. He seemed out of breath as if he were running. "But it appears someone ambushed the prison guards when they were leaving the hospital with Ogden."

Sweet heaven. "Jax, are you all right?"

"I'm fine. I wasn't there. I was on my way to the station when I got the news. I'm heading to the hospital now to see if I can pick up Ogden's trail."

"Be careful," she said, but she wasn't even sure if Jax heard her because he'd already ended the call.

"Is that there trouble?" one of the marshals asked as he walked up the steps to the porch.

At first, Addie thought he'd overheard the call from Jax, but the marshal's attention wasn't on them but rather on the black limo that was speeding up the road toward the house.

What now?

Weston didn't wait to find out. He pulled Addie away from the door and back into the family room. "Stay put," he insisted, drawing his gun again.

Jericho, Cord and both marshals did the same.

Since there was enough firepower to protect her, Addie went to the window and peeked out. And scowled. Boggs and Canales stepped out of the limo. She should have known, since there weren't many people who would arrive in a limo.

She caught a glimpse of the personalized license plate, and the first three letters were *AGB*, Boggs's initials.

"It's just me," Boggs said as if that was all that was necessary for them to put down their guns.

None of them did.

"Really? Are all those weapons necessary?" Canales snarled. "We're not criminals."

"The verdict's still out on that," Weston snarled right back. "Why are you two here?"

"Well, I tried the sheriff's office first," Boggs explained, "but the deputy said Addie, the sheriff and you were all at the ranch. We have to talk."

Again, spoken like gospel, and he started toward the porch.

"Don't come any closer," Weston warned him. "And keep your hands where I can see them."

"See?" Canales said to Boggs as if proving a point. "These people think you're a criminal, and they're treating you like one. This is what you have to stop if you want to stand a chance winning the election."

Canales shifted his attention to them. Specifically to Weston and Jericho. "You need to back off with the mud-slinging. If not, you're both going to be facing defamation-of-character lawsuits. Addie, too. She's telling lies when she should be keeping her mouth shut."

That brought her out of hiding. Not to her brothers or Weston's approval, but Addie did step in the doorway.

"I haven't lied," she insisted. "Can you say the same?"

"Of course," Canales quickly answered. Boggs stayed quiet. "I'm sure you told a boatload of lies to that Daisy Vogel. Now you've got her riled up. She called the newspaper, trying to get them to run a story about Boggs and me. Thankfully, the editor came to his senses."

More likely, the editor had been paid off by Canales, Boggs or both.

"You know where Daisy is?" Weston asked

him. There wasn't a drop of friendliness in his tone. Nor was there in the look he gave her when he took up a protective stance in front of her.

"At her house, I assume," Boggs said.

"You assume wrong. She's missing," Cord provided.

"And who are you?" Canales asked, sparing him a glance.

"Agent Cord Granger. My biological father is the Moonlight Strangler."

Clearly, neither Canales nor Boggs had been expecting that. And Addie wasn't sure it was a good idea to let these two in on that information.

"How do you know he's your father?" Canales asked, stepping closer and studying Cord. However, he stopped moving when Cord aimed his gun at him.

"I had a DNA test done." Cord's voice was calm, a discussing-the-weather tone. "I'd like for that word to get around. I'd also like for it to get around that I'm fully cooperating with the FBI so they can help me remember anything about the killer. Like his identity, for instance," he said, staring at Boggs.

*Great.* Cord was making himself bait. Maybe to protect her. But she didn't want him hurt, and it didn't matter that she'd just met him.

"How long have you known about him?" Boggs asked Addie. He tipped his head to Cord.

"Not long," she settled for saying. "How long have *you* known about him?"

Boggs jerked back his head, obviously not expecting the accusation. "I didn't know."

She believed him. But Canales was a different story. He didn't seem nearly as surprised as his boss.

"You can handle these two clowns?" Cord asked Weston. "Because I've got errands to run."

Finding Daisy was no doubt part of those "errands." They needed that to happen fast. Ditto for finding Ogden.

Cord waited until Weston had nodded before he holstered his gun and headed down the steps. "I'll be in touch," Cord said. But he paused just long enough to glance at her. "Stay safe."

"You do the same." She doubted he'd take her advice, though, especially since Cord wasn't headed to a safe house and had just set up what he no doubt hoped would be a showdown with a serial killer.

"We should be going, too," Canales insisted when Cord got in his truck and drove away. "It's obvious the only way to settle this is to go ahead and file some lawsuits."

Without taking his attention off Cord's truck, Canales went back to the limo, got in and slammed the door.

Boggs stayed put. He gave an uneasy glance

over his shoulder. "Sometimes, Ira can have a very narrow focus."

"What the hell does that mean?" Jericho snapped.

Another uneasy glance from Boggs. "He just wants to make sure that you know I'm innocent. Which I am. I wish you'd believe me so we don't have to go through with those lawsuits. That'll only keep tongues wagging."

"If you're as innocent as you claim, why don't you submit to a DNA test?" Weston asked.

Boggs looked just as surprised about that as he had Cord's revelation. "Why would I do that?"

"To prove you're not the Moonlight Strangler."

That seemed to tighten every muscle in Boggs's body. "I refuse to be a suspect in any of this."

"You can refuse all you want, but you're a suspect whether you call yourself one or not," Weston informed him. "Tell me about the gunrunning that was operating over in Comal County thirty years ago. When you're finished, convince me that your uncle wasn't a dirty coroner on the take."

Boggs cursed and his eyes narrowed. "You're making some very dangerous assumptions, Ranger Cade."

"That's not convincing me you're innocent," Weston told him. "How much do you know?"

The look Boggs gave him could have frozen

the Sahara. "I know nothing," he insisted, and he stormed toward the limo and got inside.

Almost immediately, the driver took off. Addie and the others stayed there, watching until the car was away from the house.

Once it was out of sight, the marshals came onto the porch. "By the way, I'm Daniel Seaver," the bulkier man said. "This is Kirk Vance. And we should get going to the safe house before you get another round of visitors who shouldn't be here."

Weston introduced them to Addie, and then told her that he'd get her suitcase from her room upstairs.

Jericho looked back at her. "Your brother's either an idiot or he has a death wish."

Addie was thinking it was definitely the latter.

"You're my brother," she reminded Jericho. Something she wanted to clear up right away. "I'm not sure what Cord is to me yet, but I have room for one more if it comes down to it."

The corner of Jericho's mouth twitched. "You're sure about that? That's not what you used to tell Jax, Chase, Levi and me when you were a kid. You always said you had way too many brothers."

They shared a smile. Since Jericho was more of the scowling type, Addie took it as the rare gift that it was. From a brother she loved.

Weston came back downstairs, his bag in one hand. Hers in the other.

"You'll be okay?" Jericho asked her. "You won't take any stupid chances." That last one wasn't a question.

She nodded. But Jericho took his brotherly/sheriff duties one step further. "Take care of her," Jericho said like a warning to Weston.

"I will."

Normally, Addie would have balked at her brother taking charge of her. And of Weston accepting the handoff. But after everything that'd happened, she was willing to take all the security she could get.

Like the other times they'd been outside, Weston got her moving as quickly as possible to the car, and they got in the backseat with the marshals in the front. Marshal Seaver didn't waste any time getting them on the road. When Addie looked back at the house, Jericho was already talking on the phone. No doubt trying to end this danger so she could come home.

Of course, that would be just the start of yet another hurdle.

With Weston.

The baby was still months from being born, but they would need to make arrangements and set some ground rules. Too bad she had no idea what kind of ground rules to put in place. Or if they'd even do any good. Her body seemed to have its own rules when it came to Weston.

"You know the drill," Seaver said to Weston. "I'll have to drive around until I'm sure we aren't being followed. You might want to grab a nap," he added to her.

Addie thanked him, but no way would that happen. She was exhausted, but her mind was whirling with everything she'd just learned. Still, she closed her eyes and hoped to settle down the nerves. It didn't work until Weston slid his arm around her and eased her against him so she could use his shoulder as a pillow.

Yes, her body definitely had its own notions when it came to Weston.

She could almost feel the tension drain from her. It didn't last, though. They'd only been on the road for fifteen minutes or so when Weston's phone buzzed, jarring her nerves right back to the surface.

"Sorry." Weston moved away from her so he could take his phone from his pocket.

"Put it on speaker," she insisted when she saw Jax's name on the screen.

"I decided to make this a conference call with Jericho," Jax greeted, "so I could update you all at the same time."

While Addie was all for getting updates, she knew from her brother's tone that he was about to deliver more bad news. She tried to brace herself for it and prayed that Cord's challenge to the killer hadn't led to some kind of violent confrontation.

"The cops went to McCain's house, and he wasn't there," Jax explained. "There were signs of a struggle. Some blood, too."

*No.* She'd been sure if they could find the lawyer that he'd eventually give them some info that would lead them to the Moonlight Strangler. Or at least to the person who'd actually hired him.

"Someone's tying up loose ends," Weston grumbled. "Unless the scene was staged."

"Not likely on the staged part. Too much blood for that, and there were some expensive paintings and such that had been damaged. But SAPD did manage to get something from McCain's computer records."

SAPD. San Antonio Police Department. "What did they find?" she asked her brother.

"McCain has done legal work for both Canales and Boggs."

That didn't surprise her at all, and it gave them a connection between them and Ogden since McCain was Ogden's lawyer, too.

"Any idea which one of them hired McCain to represent Ogden?" Weston pressed, taking the question right out of her mouth.

"It's hard to tell. The payment for representing Ogden came from an offshore account. There are layers and layers of cover so it might be impossible to find out who actually owns that account. The FBI is on it, so maybe they'll get something."

Maybe, but that seemed like a long shot. If either Canales or Boggs had set this up in advance, then they'd no doubt make sure it couldn't be linked back to them.

"We need to find Ogden," Jericho snapped. "He's the key to sorting this out. Hell, he could be the owner of that offshore account."

"Could be, but there's a problem with that." Jax huffed. "It appears Ogden didn't cooperate with the escape. I used the word *appears* because he could have been faking it, but he was yelling for help when the men took him. And one of the guys punched him."

That caused Jericho to curse. Addie wanted to do the same. If Ogden was a loose end that was about to be *tied up*, then there went one of their best chances of linking him to the killer.

"There's more," Jax said.

"Good news, I hope," Addie mumbled.

"Not really. Well, it's good news for Canales. We did a rush on his DNA test, and he's not the Moonlight Strangler."

"You're sure?" she asked.

"I'm sure unless Canales somehow managed to tamper with the test. That would mean he has an insider at the lab. Possible, I suppose. That's why I'm having another test run at a different lab."

Good. Addie figured a man like Canales could—and would—tamper with potential evidence.

"Wait a sec," Jericho said, "I got another call coming in. It's from Cord."

That instantly put a knot in her stomach. From the sound of Jericho's voice, he had a similar reaction. But his reaction probably wasn't because he was afraid for Cord's life.

Unlike the conference call, Addie couldn't hear what Cord was saying because Jericho had put them on hold. Jax, Weston and she just waited. And waited. With that knot tightening even more.

"If Cord's calling," Weston reminded her, "then he's all right."

True. That was something at least. But she doubted he'd stay all right if he continued to taunt a killer.

It seemed to take an eternity for Jericho to come back on the line, and even when he did, he didn't jump right into an explanation about Cord's call.

"What's wrong?" she asked.

"It's Daisy," Jericho finally said. "The cops found her. Addie, I'm sorry, but she's dead."

# *Chapter Thirteen*

Daisy was dead. *Murdered.* According to Jax, she'd been strangled and had that obscene, too familiar crescent-shaped cut on her cheek.

The signature of the Moonlight Strangler.

Definitely not the way Weston had wanted this to go. Even if it turned out Daisy was involved in the attacks against Addie, Weston had wanted her alive so she could talk. Now they'd lost that chance along with perhaps an innocent woman losing her life.

That meant the danger to Addie was just as great as it had been two days earlier. And worse, she was beyond shaken. The moment they'd arrived at the safe house, she had gone to her room. Probably not to rest, but Weston had pretended that was happening so she could have some time to try to come to terms with all of this.

If that was possible.

Maybe the shower she was taking now would help. Since she'd been in there a good half hour,

Weston figured she was in there crying. Or cursing their situation.

Maybe both.

Even though he was across the hall in another bedroom, they'd left their doors open, and he heard her phone ding. Not her usual phone but a safe, untraceable one that the marshals had given her to use. The only people who had the number were members of her family. Since the phone was on the nightstand, he went in her room to have a look. It was from Jericho.

You okay? her brother texted. Just checking.

Too bad Jericho hadn't texted with good news. That might improve Addie's mood.

Or not.

She stepped out of the bathroom, her attention going right to him. For just a second he saw the emotions and the hurt in her eyes before she did her best to shut down. She failed.

Yeah, there wasn't much that was going to help with her mood.

She was dressed, thank goodness, in jeans and a dark green top. Weston figured his mind was already in a bad place, and it sure wouldn't have helped if a naked Addie had come walking out of the bathroom. Of course, she likely wouldn't have done that since there were two other marshals in the house.

Addie went to the window and glanced outside.

Not that there was much for her to see. The safe house was located in the middle of nowhere with no other houses around for miles.

Once, it'd been a small working ranch, but now the barn and pastures were empty. Ditto for the road leading to the place. There'd been no traffic the entire week prior to their arrivals, and the marshals knew that because a motion-activated security sensor had been fitted to one of the trees right off the road. If anyone tried to get to the place on foot or by car, Daniel and Kirk would be alerted.

"I hope we don't have to be here for Christmas," she said under her breath.

Heck, he hoped so, too, since Christmas was nearly three weeks away. He wanted the danger over and done with well before that.

"Jericho just texted you." Weston tipped his head to the phone and sank down on the edge of her bed. "He wants to know if you're okay."

She made a soft as-if sound, but she did send a text with their now routine lie, to say that yes, she was okay.

"It's my fault Daisy's dead," Addie said as soon as she finished the text.

Weston huffed. "And how do you figure that?"

Her hair was wet, her face rosy and damp from the shower, and when she walked closer to him, he caught the scent of a floral shampoo.

And her own scent, too, swirling beneath it.

Hard to miss those scents when she sat down next to him. Much too close. Of course, maybe a mile was too close when it came to Addie.

"I should have made Daisy understand the danger she was in," Addie finally answered.

"Because of your ESP, right?"

She frowned at his attempted humor.

"Daisy knew the risks when she sneaked out of the hospital," Weston added. "She could have just stayed in protective custody with one of your brothers. She didn't. She ran. And in my experience, innocent people don't run from the law."

"Maybe..."

She was no doubt about to launch into stage two of a guilt fest that wouldn't do her or the baby any good. So Weston put a stop to it.

By kissing her.

Of course, that didn't fix anything. Addie pulled back, looking surprised, confused and maybe a couple of other emotions he didn't want to identify.

"Bad idea, I know," he said before she could say it.

But Addie didn't say it. She just stared at him for a few seconds, then slid her hand around his neck to pull him back to her.

And she kissed him.

Okay, so maybe not such a bad idea after all. Or perhaps they were both making a mistake. One touch of his mouth to hers though, and Weston didn't care how many mistakes they made.

This was the heat he'd felt with her in that San Antonio hotel.

The instant fire mixed with the slam of sensations. Her mouth, her touch.

*Her.*

And just like those others times, Weston felt himself falling. Touching, too. Because obviously his crazy body thought he hadn't screwed this up enough so he hauled her closer and closer. Until she was practically in his lap.

There was a serious problem with kisses this good. They only upped an already too hot heat. Ditto for the touching. His hand landed on her breasts. Then under her top so that bare skin was on bare skin.

The heat went up a notch.

Weston quit thinking about notches, however, when he lowered his head, shoved down her bra and kissed her there. Actually, he quit thinking about everything and just kept taking.

Addie was taking, too. Fumbling with his buttons. Putting her hand inside his shirt and on his chest.

Then lower.

That's when Weston took hold of the tiny grain of sanity he had left. He didn't let go of her, but he got them to their feet, and, without breaking the kisses and touches, he maneuvered them to the door so he could close it.

They didn't make it back to the bed, though.

Addie pushed him against the door, pinning him in place. Not that he needed to be pinned. Weston had no plans to go anywhere unless it was to drag her to the floor.

So that's what he did.

More sanity returned when she reached for his zipper. Oh, man. He really wanted what she clearly had in mind, but talk about bad timing. Bad everything. This was probably some kind of adrenaline crash reaction that Addie would regret later.

Weston doubted he could talk any part of his body into regret.

Still, he had to think of her. Had to give her a breather so she could try to consider all of this with a clear head.

Or not.

She cursed him when he tried to stop her, and that's when Weston realized they'd taken this past the point of no return. Well, for her anyway.

He shoved down her zipper and slipped his hand inside her panties. All right. He had to grind his teeth together to keep himself from saying something stupid.

Like—*let's do this now.*

They would do something, but he had to keep some shred of sanity. If he was inside her, no sanity.

She was still struggling with him, to make this a round of old-fashioned sex. Good sex, no doubt. But Addie stopped when he sank his fingers inside her.

Clamping her teeth over her bottom lip, she didn't make a sound. Didn't look at him. But, man, the pleasure was there all over her face.

Pleasure for him, too.

It didn't take much for him to finish things for her. Probably because those kisses had put her right at the brink. It only took a few strokes, and Weston saw—and felt—her shatter.

Now she made a sound. A sharp moan that tugged at him. Well, it tugged at one very hard part of him anyway, and that idiot part of him started to suggest some bad things.

"Everything okay in there, Addie?" Seaver called out a split second before Weston heard the marshal's footsteps making their way down the hall toward them.

Addie gasped and scrambled away from him. Not easily. Especially since she was trying to fix her top and jeans.

"We're fine," Weston lied for her. "Any news?"

"Jericho might have a lead on Lonny Ogden. If anything comes of it, I'll let you know." The marshal reversed his steps and went back toward the front of the house.

"Good grief," Addie said under her breath.

Weston hated that she looked embarrassed. "I've seen you stark naked, and I've kissed nearly every inch of you, remember? This was like second base."

"Third," she corrected, making him chuckle.

There was a hint of that humor he missed. Addie hadn't exactly been cracking jokes during their time in San Antonio, but there'd been moments when she had managed to keep things light.

She didn't move closer to him but glanced at his very noticeable zipper region. "Should I do something about that?"

Weston gave her a blank stare. "I'm a man. The answer to that question is usually a yes. *Usually*," he emphasized. "But I'm thinking you've got five minutes tops before the climax wears off and you come to your senses."

It didn't take her anywhere near five minutes. More like five seconds. "You're right. Sorry." She finished fixing her clothes. "Sex is a complication I don't need right now."

It hit him then. The baby. Something that hadn't been on his mind when his hand had been in her panties. "Is what we did okay? I mean for the baby?"

Now she was the one giving the flat look. "The

baby is fine. Pregnant women can and obviously do have climaxes. As you just proved." She actually blushed. "Maybe talking is safer," she grumbled.

No doubt, but he figured that meant Addie would go back to discussing Daisy, the attacks or the killer.

She stared at him. "Are you ever going to tell me why you never wanted to have children?"

Okay, not a question he especially wanted on the conversation table. Still, maybe it was better than talking about sex or murder.

*Maybe.*

Or maybe he was just playing with a different kind of fire.

Addie was clearly waiting for an answer, but it took Weston a while to find one he could manage. "My father didn't abandon me the way yours did, but I wish he had."

She stayed quiet a moment. "Did he have something to do with the scars on your back?" The flat look returned when he just stared at her. "I've seen every inch of you naked, too. You have at least a dozen scars on your back."

Yeah, those. He always lied about them, saying they were rodeo injuries, but it didn't seem right to lie to Addie. "My dad was a mean drunk, and my mother did whatever she could to make sure she wasn't the one on the receiving end of his fists and his belt."

Addie glanced away, swallowed hard. "My father gave you the other scar. The one on your chest." She touched her cheek. "Both of us have lots of scars. Some visible, some not."

Weston leaned toward her. "I gave you one of those invisible scars. A broken heart." He touched her heart. At least that was his intention, but it also meant touching her breast.

She didn't exactly skitter away from him. "Who gave you your broken heart?" She leaned over, brushed her fingers over his chest and sent a nice trickle of heat through him.

"Amy Wilkins. Tenth grade."

But he knew that wasn't what she wanted to hear. No. This was the talk. *The* one he'd never had with anyone.

"I wasn't in love with Collette," he said. There, it was like ripping off a bandage. It hurt like hell, but the wound was there for Addie to see.

"W-what?" Obviously, it wasn't a confession she'd expected.

"I tried to love her," Weston explained, "but I knew I couldn't give her the life she wanted. So I went to her office that night to break things off with her. Instead, I walked in on her being murdered."

"Oh, God," she whispered.

Weston had repeated that a couple of thousand times since her murder. Along with wanting to punish himself.

"Did she know you didn't love her?" Addie asked.

"Considering I'd never said those words to her, I'm pretty sure she knew."

Addie made a sound of surprise. "You never told her you loved her?"

"Before I met you in San Antonio, I didn't make it a habit of lying to people." He let that hang in the air between them. "Obviously, lying didn't work out so well."

She didn't argue with that and probably wouldn't have even if her phone hadn't rung. "It's likely one of my brothers checking on me." She got up and went to the nightstand.

Then, she froze.

"It says unknown caller on the screen," Addie said, her gaze flying back to him.

Weston couldn't get to the phone fast enough. He hit the answer button and put it on speaker.

"Hello, Addie," the caller said. It was a man, and Weston didn't recognize his voice. "We need to talk."

"Who is this?" she asked. "And how did you get my number?"

"I got it from your brother Chase. Rather, I got it from his phone. Don't worry. He's all right. Or at least he will be once the effects of the stun gun have worn off. Funny thing about brothers. Even adopted ones. They don't like to share information about their kid sister."

Hell. Weston hurried to door, threw it open and called out for the marshals. "Make sure Addie's brother Chase is all right and try to trace the call she just got."

Daniel nodded and took out his own phone. The other marshal did the same.

"Who is this?" Addie repeated, her voice shaking now.

"You don't know? Well, let's just keep it formal, okay? You can call me the Moonlight Strangler."

Addie froze. Her eyes, widened. Her breath stalled in her throat.

"How do we know you're who you say you are?" Weston demanded.

"Ahh, Ranger Cade. You're one of those devil-in-the-details kind of people. Well, here's my proof. I cut all my ladies on their cheeks. That's not in any of the reports, is it, Ranger Cade?

No, it wasn't. But it wasn't enough. "Convince me. Give me something else."

"No wonder you and Addie have a thing for each other. Like minds and all that. All right. Here's your something else. I took Leta's necklace. A little gold angel. I'm sure in the reports her brother said she wore it all the time and that it was the only thing missing when her body turned up."

Weston nodded when Addie looked at him. None of the other victims had been missing any jewelry or items of clothing.

"Chase is okay," Daniel relayed to them. "His phone was stolen, but I reached him through a fellow marshal who's on the scene with him now." Then he shook his head. "We can't trace the killer's call. He's using a prepaid cell."

Of course he was. This snake had avoided capture for thirty years or more. However, he'd taken a huge risk going after Chase. Addie's brother was a marshal and might have seen or heard something that could help them identify him.

Addie took a short breath of relief before turning her attention back to the phone. "Who are you?" Addie demanded. "And by that, I mean what's your name?"

He made a *tsk-tsk* sound. "Wouldn't do to tell you that. Jail's no place for me."

"Then tell me about my birth mother."

Weston hadn't expected the question, but the Moonlight Strangler obviously had. "She's dead," he answered without hesitation.

Addie put her hand over her heart, no doubt to try to steady it. "Did you kill her?"

"Yes." Another quick admission. "But she won't

be on your list of victims. Sometimes, it's best if I don't show off my work."

Her bottom lip started to tremble, and she had to clamp her teeth over it for a few seconds. "You're insane."

"Possibly. But I do have my own personal code of conduct, and I'm not the one after you."

Like Weston, he could see Addie replaying that in her head. Did she believe him? Not a chance. But anything this guy could tell them might help them catch him.

"Then who is after me?" she asked.

"Secrets, secrets," the man taunted.

Hell. Weston wanted to reach through the phone and strangle this idiot. Since he couldn't do that and because punching walls wouldn't be very productive, he went in another direction.

"Did you send me a letter that threatened my sister?" Weston asked him.

"Not me. Your sister is of no interest to me."

"You're sure about that? I've been working damn hard to find you, and you could want to get back at me."

"I wouldn't have expected anything less from you. It's the reason I don't go after lawmen. Too persistent. Persistence got Addie's sister-in-law in trouble, didn't it? By the way, how's your brother doing?"

That didn't help the color in Addie's cheeks.

"Paige," she said under her breath. "And how do you think my brother's doing?" She had a lot more volume in her voice when she asked that. "You murdered his wife."

"His ex-wife," the man corrected.

Weston knew the details of Paige's murder. Too many details. The kind that made it hard for him to sleep at night. The kind that'd no doubt given Addie and especially her brother Jax plenty of nightmares. This monster had taken way too much from the Crocketts.

"Paige's death couldn't be helped," he said as if that excused everything. "If it makes you feel better, she's the only one I regret. Tell your brother that."

"Jax won't ever hear that from me," she snapped. "Because I don't believe it for a minute. I doubt you're even capable of feeling regret."

"You're wrong." He paused again. "But we're getting off topic again, and I need to end this call soon."

"Not until you give us some answers," Weston insisted.

"All right. Here's an answer, Ranger Cade. You're of no interest to me. Addie, well, she's of interest only because we're family."

The anger fired through her eyes. "You're not my family."

He chuckled. "A sensitive topic, I see."

Weston was tired of dealing with this. “Tell us who’s after Addie and why.”

“Secrets, secrets,” he repeated. “There’s a big surprise planned for you.”

“Quit playing games.” Weston added some profanity to that.

“But games are *so* much fun. But I will say this—if you want to stop him, then make sure Addie remembers all about her time with Daisy. I’m not the only one with secrets.”

“Daisy’s dead. Your doing?” Weston asked.

“Hardly. Not my type. Not like Collette and the others.”

“I wasn’t your type,” Weston reminded him after he got past the mental punch to the gut at hearing the killer say Collette’s name, “and you left me for dead.”

“You got in the way. If you’re not careful, the same will happen when he comes after Addie.”

*“He?”* Addie and Weston questioned together. “Give me a name,” Weston demanded.

A very long silence.

“All right. Here’s a name. Lonny Ogden. I’m pretty sure he’s trying to pull a copycat.”

Finally. But Weston had no idea if it was the truth or if the Moonlight Strangler was just playing more games.

“Did you put Ogden up to coming after me?” Addie asked.

"No way. I take pride in what I do, and Lonny-boy's a sloppy mess. My own fault, though."

Weston didn't like the sound of that. "What do you mean?"

"I mean..." The killer didn't jump to finish that until he'd made them wait several moments. "I'm responsible for creating Lonny-boy. It's my blood running through his veins."

And with that, he laughed and ended the call.

## *Chapter Fourteen*

Addie hadn't realized just how weak her legs had gotten until she felt Weston hook his arm around her waist. He had her sit on the bed, his attention immediately going to Daniel.

Her mind was whirling. As if a tornado had gotten inside her head. She'd actually heard the voice of the Moonlight Strangler. Chase had been attacked. Her birth mother was dead.

If the killer was telling the truth.

"Is there any chance the Moonlight Strangler can use that phone number to find the location of the safe house?" Weston asked the marshals.

Oh, God. That put her heart right back in her throat. She hadn't even considered that.

"No," Daniel assured them. "Each of Addie's family members was given the phone number but not the address."

Good. That was something at least, but it didn't get her heart out of her throat. Mercy, when was this going to end?

"We had DNA tests run on Ogden, and they should be back in a day or two," Weston explained to Daniel. "Jericho and the FBI will need to know about this, too."

"And Chase," Addie added. "I need to talk to Chase."

Daniel had already said that Chase was all right, but she wanted to hear her brother's voice, to make sure he wasn't trying to shield her. Things were already bad enough, but if her brother had been hurt...well, she didn't want to go there.

The marshals both stepped out in the hall to make the calls, but they didn't go far. Definitely not letting her out their sight. Of course, Weston wasn't leaving, either. He sat next to her, pulling her into his arms.

"Ogden is my brother?" she asked.

"The killer could have been lying about that," Weston reminded her.

True. But why would he do that?

*It's my blood running through his veins.*

And that meant it was the same blood running through hers.

"I didn't feel any kind of connection to him," she added. "Unlike Cord. I felt something there."

Plus, there'd been the memory of the brown bear.

"Ogden's probably crazy," Weston went on. "And I don't mean he just acts crazy. He might truly be insane along with being a Moonlight

Strangler groupie. Ogden maybe somehow convinced the killer that he was his son so he could deepen whatever connection he thinks is between them."

Perhaps. But the killer didn't seem to be someone who could easily be convinced of anything, especially a lie.

Weston caught her chin, lifted it, forcing eye contact with her. "The good news is the killer said he wasn't the one after you. If that's true—and I think it might be—then all of this makes a lot more sense."

She had to shake her head. "None of this makes sense."

"But it does. You've known for three months that the Moonlight Strangler is your biological father. I kept going back to the question—if he wanted you silenced, then why hadn't he come after you sooner? If I could just walk onto the ranch, then he could have, too. He didn't."

Addie couldn't argue with that, but she did see a problem. "The same could be said of a copycat. Why now?"

"Maybe it has to do with Cord."

All right. That got her attention.

"Cord found out he was a DNA match about the same time the attacks on you started," Weston continued. "Someone might not want you teaming up with your brother and recalling any shared memories."

Since that'd already happened, then it was a valid fear. But the problem was neither Cord nor she had remembered anything incriminating about anyone.

"I've got your brother Chase on the line," Daniel interrupted.

Addie couldn't get to his phone fast enough. "Are you okay?" she asked Chase right away.

"I'm fine. How about you?"

Her brother didn't sound fine. He sounded shaken up. And riled. Addie knew exactly how he felt. "I'm worried about you."

"Don't be. I was just zapped when I got out of my car to interview a witness. Nothing to do with the Moonlight Strangler. This is all my fault, really. I was distracted, and I didn't see the stun gun in the woman's hand until it was too late."

"A woman?" Weston asked.

"Yeah. She looked as if she'd been attacked. Clothes torn. Hair a mess. She staggered toward me, and when I reached for her, she hit me with a stun gun. When I came to, I was facedown in the parking lot and my phone was missing."

Addie felt the chill snake down her spine. Chase could have been killed, and she was betting the reason he was distracted was because he was worried about her. "Any idea who the woman was?"

"None. I'll check for any surveillance cameras, but I figure she was just a lackey. Maybe even a homeless person hired to do the job. Don't worry. I'll be more careful. You do the same."

There was an alert that another call was coming in, so Addie told her brother goodbye and handed the phone back to Daniel. Daniel cursed as soon as he saw the screen.

"It's an unknown caller again," Daniel told them.

At the same moment, there was a text from Jericho on Weston's phone.

Ogden is about to call you, Jericho texted Weston. Call me after you've talked to him.

Addie was actually relieved it was Ogden. She wasn't sure she was up for another round with the Moonlight Strangler when she hadn't recovered from their initial conversation. But, of course, talking to Ogden wouldn't exactly be a picnic.

Especially after what she'd just learned.

*It's my blood running through his veins.*

"Marshal Seaver, don't hang up," Ogden greeted. "I've been calling all over the place, and that rude sheriff in Appaloosa Pass finally gave me your number. I need to speak to Ranger Cade right now. He's not answering his phone, and I'm betting you know how to get in touch with him."

Weston wasn't answering his phone because, like Addie's, his had been left at the ranch and swapped out with ones that couldn't be tracked. They certainly hadn't given Ogden their new numbers.

"I'm listening," Weston said, moving closer to the phone. "Where the hell are you?"

"As if I'd tell you. The sheriff kept asking me the same thing, and I'll say to you what I said to him. You won't find me unless I want to be found. And I don't want to be found right now."

"Really?" Weston fired back. "Because I heard you were kicking and screaming when those men took you from the hospital. Was that all an act?"

"No!" His voice was a screech. "I have no idea who they were, and I got away as soon as I could."

"You managed to escape with that injury?" Weston sounded as skeptical as Addie felt. Because Ogden could be lying, not only about this but anything else he told them.

"Yes, I did. I'm resourceful when I have to be. But there's a problem. I managed to get to a computer to access the security feed I set up around my apartment."

Daniel looked at Weston, silently asking if he knew about the feed, and Weston shook his head. If Weston and the other lawmen hadn't seen cameras, then they were well hidden.

"There are cops in my apartment," Ogden went on, "and I want you to tell them to get out. I can't hear what they're saying, but I can see them going through everything. I don't want them touching my things."

Good grief. That was his biggest concern right now? Maybe Weston was right about Ogden being insane. Or else this was Ogden's way of trying to make them believe he was. That way, if he was caught, he could be looking at time in a mental hospital instead of jail.

"There's an easy fix to this problem," Weston snarled. "If you want the cops out, just turn yourself in, and give them whatever it is they're looking for."

"You know I can't do that. You'll arrest me."

"Yeah, I will, but the alternative is you dying while on the run. I take it your kidnapper didn't have friendly intentions toward you?"

"No." For one word, it carried a lot of emotion. Mainly anger. "They wanted me to do things I didn't want to do."

"Like what?" Weston pressed when Ogden didn't continue.

"I'm not after Addie. Not anymore. I don't want her dead, and I didn't have anything to do with that stuff that went on at that old lady's house."

"Really? You're not after Addie? Convince me."

That was Weston's favorite order. *Convince me.* Something she doubted Ogden could do.

Ogden made a sound of disapproval, clearly not pleased with Weston's sarcasm. "I can't, not over the phone. But if you get those cops out of my place, I'll turn myself in so we can talk face-to-face. I'll be able to convince Addie and you."

She wasn't holding her breath about that.

"Give me some time," Weston finally said. "I'll see if I can help."

"You don't believe he'd turn himself in," Addie protested when Weston ended the call and reached for his own phone.

"No. But obviously there's something in that apartment that Ogden doesn't want them to find."

While the marshals were busy with their own calls, Weston worked his way through several people in SAPD before he was finally connected to an officer, Detective Riley Jenkins, on the scene of the search of Ogden's apartment.

"Just got a call from Ogden, and he claims to be watching you via remote camera access," Weston told the detective. "He also says he'll turn himself in if you and your team leave the apartment. He won't, of course, but he might be stupid enough to try to get into his place to retrieve whatever it is he's worried about you finding."

"I think we've already found it," Jenkins answered in a whisper.

Addie felt a too familiar punch of dread. She doubted there was anything in Ogden's apartment that would put her at ease.

"Hold on while I step outside," the detective

added. It only took a few moments for him to come back on the line. "I'm not sure if Ogden has audio, but I didn't want to risk it. We found the cameras shortly after we got in."

"Does Ogden know that?" Weston asked.

"Oh, yes. We've blocked the one we found in the bedroom. I'm sure that's got him running scared. He's been calling all over, looking for someone who can get us out of here, and I'm hoping he'll panic and try to move us out of here himself. We're ready for an attack. Ready to catch him and put him back in jail where he belongs."

Good. Because Ogden sounded as if he was at a breaking point.

"What'd you find?" Weston asked.

"Plenty. I'm texting you a picture of something we saw in his bedroom."

Addie pressed her fingers to her mouth and prayed that it wasn't another dead body. But it wasn't. As the picture loaded, it took her a while to figure out exactly what she was seeing. There were newspaper clippings taped to the walls. Dozens, maybe even hundreds of them. And from what she could tell, all the clippings were articles about the Moonlight Strangler.

"It's like a shrine," the detective went on. "In addition to the stuff on the walls, he has folders from where he's printed out blog posts and anything that mentions the killer. That's where we found the letters from the Moonlight Strangler."

Letters. Ogden hadn't mentioned those.

"You think they're real?" Weston asked.

"At least one of them is. It's typed, no envelope so we don't have a postmark, but there's a detail in it that only the killer would know. It has to do with a necklace and one of the victims."

Leta's necklace.

But that immediately gave Addie an uneasy feeling.

That was the same item the Moonlight Strangler had offered them as proof of his identity. Was it possible that someone like Canales or Boggs had gotten access to that detail and was using it to manipulate Ogden?

If so, had that really been the Moonlight Strangler who'd just called her? Or maybe someone was just playing sick games with her.

"The letter's an apology, and it's dated about three months ago," Jenkins explained. "The Strangler tells Ogden he's sorry for not being there for him, that he knows Ogden had a tough life. And he did. When Ogden was three, he was adopted by a couple who used him as a punching bag. Lots of trips to the ER for broken bones and such."

Addie hadn't known that about Ogden, and it almost made her feel sorry for him. *Almost.*

"His adoptive parents were both killed in a car accident and left him a nice trust fund," Jenkins added, "but I'm sure that doesn't make up for the abuse."

No. Nothing could make up for something like that. But a trust fund meant Ogden had access to money that he could have used to hire the hit man who tried to kill her.

"Did the Moonlight Strangler say anything about being Ogden's biological father?" Weston asked. It was the exact question on Addie's mind.

"Not outright, but he implied it," the detective said without hesitating. "Apparently, you'd already put in a DNA test on Ogden so I just called about fifteen minutes ago and got the results."

"The test is back?" Weston said, giving her a long look. He also put his arm around her. "And?"

"It's a match."

Addie felt the air swoosh out of her. This wouldn't have been easy no matter what, but it was a hard pill to swallow that her own brother had wanted her dead.

"The lab compared Ogden's DNA to the Moonlight Strangler's biological daughter, Addie Crockett, and although it's not a full sibling match, the DNA does prove that Ogden is her half-brother. Same paternal DNA, different mother, though."

Weston jumped right on that. "Any idea who that mother is?"

"No. Her DNA's not in the system."

Which meant she didn't have a criminal record. It was also possible that she was still alive.

Unlike Addie's own birth mother.

If she was to believe the killer, then her birth mother had been one of his victims. But maybe not Ogden's mother. And if the woman was alive, she might be able to give them the identity of the Moonlight Strangler. Of course, that would mean finding her, but maybe Ogden could help with that.

"Thanks," Weston told Jenkins. "If Ogden shows up or if you find anything else, let me know. Addie Crockett's life could depend on it."

The detective assured him that he would, and they ended the call.

"He's really my brother," Addie managed to say.

Weston stared at her. "No. Don't go there. Ogden's DNA didn't make him the way he is. You heard what the detective said about the abuse."

She had, and Addie had no choice but to latch on to it. But there was something else bothering her about this.

"Ogden's thirty-one. Cord and I are thirty-three," she explained. "Jenkins said Ogden wasn't adopted until he was three, and that means he was a year old when Cord and I were abandoned. So where was Ogden during those two years before he was adopted? With his birth mother or with our sick excuse for a father?"

Weston shook his head and took out his phone again. "I don't know, but I'll see what I can find out. If the adoption was legal, then maybe I can get the records unsealed and go from there."

However, Weston didn't get a chance to make the call because another one came in, and Addie saw Jericho's name on the screen.

"I just heard about Ogden's test results," Jericho said the moment Weston answered the phone. "Is Addie okay?"

She opened her mouth to tell him yes, but the lie stuck in her throat. "I'm dealing with it," she settled for saying.

Jericho cursed. "I'm sorry. If there's anything I could do to make this go away, I'd do it."

"I know you would." Weston would, too. The only bright spot in all of this was the lawmen who would protect both her baby and her with their lives.

But Addie prayed it didn't come down to that.

"I just got off the phone with the FBI," Jericho continued a moment later. "I'm not sure I like their idea, but they're insisting this is the best way to try to recover your lost memories."

"The best way?" she asked at the same moment that Weston said, "What are you talking about?"

"More hypnosis," Jericho said after taking a

long breath. "But this time, they want to do the session at Daisy's house. Addie, they want you there tomorrow."

## *Chapter Fifteen*

A dead woman's house was one of the last places Weston wanted Addie to be.

But he could see the rationale behind bringing her here. The place had triggered the memory of the swing set, and maybe it would trigger something else.

Especially since they were practically at a dead end in the investigation.

Ogden was still on the loose, and there were no adoption records for him. No birth certificate, either. Added to that, there was no concrete evidence to get search warrants for Canales and Boggs. In fact, Boggs was still fighting the request for his DNA on the grounds that he didn't want to be any part of the investigation into the Moonlight Strangler.

Of course, Boggs was also claiming that he was still looking for the killer, but Weston wasn't buying Boggs's claim that it was all to avenge a childhood friend's murder. There was something else going on.

Something Addie might remember.

However, at the moment she didn't look any more comfortable with this than Weston was. Her nerves had been sky-high on the drive over, and seeing the house hadn't helped, either. Probably because someone had tried to murder her there just the day before.

Weston had to make sure that didn't happen again.

There were five lawmen at Daisy's house—including her brother Jericho the two marshals and Appaloosa Pass deputy Dexter Conway. Addie had been escorted in while wearing a Kevlar vest, and she'd leave the same way.

But it was this middle part of the visit that was no doubt causing the most alarm in her eyes.

"It'll be okay," Weston tried to assure her.

The assurance sucked, and the kiss he brushed on her forehead earned him a glare from Jericho. Weston ignored him and gave her a quick kiss on the mouth before stepping away so the therapist, Dr. Melissa Grinstead, could get to work.

Since the pregnancy prevented the doctor from administering any drugs, she had Addie lying on the bed in the guest room. The door, both windows and the blinds were closed, and while the room wasn't exactly pitch-dark, it was close thanks to the room being on the east side of the house. The late afternoon sun wasn't threading much light inside.

Dr. Grinstead had already warned Jericho and Weston that while they could remain in the room, they weren't allowed to say anything.

No matter what.

Weston figured that meant Addie might remember some things she didn't exactly want to remember. The stuff of nightmares.

The doctor's voice was soft and soothing, and for several minutes she just talked to Addie, telling her how to breathe and to think of relaxing things, like a running creek and warm sunlight.

Addie's eyes drifted down, and Weston finally saw the tension ease from her body. Surprisingly, it stayed that way even though the therapist began to ask her questions about her childhood, and she didn't use Addie's name but rather called her Gabrielle.

"Think back," the therapist prompted. "Do you remember being in this house when you were a little girl?"

"There's a swing set outside," Addie readily answered.

"Did you play on it?"

Addie smiled. A child's smile. "Lots."

"Were you alone?" the doctor asked.

No smile this time. “Sometimes. Davy’s not with me.”

The therapist glanced back at Weston and Jericho to see if they knew who that was, but they shook their heads.

“Who’s Davy?” Dr. Grinstead continued.

“My brother. He didn’t come to the lady’s house with me. I wanted him to come so he could push me in the swing.”

Addie was likely talking about Cord since Ogden would have been too young.

“Do you remember your whole name?” the doctor continued.

“Gabby-elle.” She said it the way a child might, and that was it. No surname. Of course, these were the memories of a three-year-old.

“What about your parents? Do you know their names?” The therapist was obviously trying a different angle.

One that didn’t work. “Mama and Daddy,” Addie answered. “But Mama’s gone.”

“Gone where?”

Good question. Especially since the person claiming to be the Moonlight Strangler had said he’d killed her birth mother.

“Don’t know,” Addie finally said, and Weston didn’t think it was his imagination that there was sadness in her voice. Maybe that meant she’d loved her mother. Didn’t all kids?

Well, except for him.

"Where's your daddy?" the doctor tried again.

"Don't know. The man brought me to the lady and said I was to stay until Daddy came back."

"And did he come back?"

Addie squeezed her eyes shut even tighter. Hell, Weston hoped she wasn't remembering something god-awful.

"Don't know," she repeated.

It was both a relief and frustrating. If she had remembered her father returning, then she might have been able to give them a description, but she might have also remembered a murder or two.

"Tell me about the lady you stayed with," Dr. Grinstead continued. "Was she here alone with you, or were there other people in the house?"

"Sometimes, we were alone." Addie's forehead bunched up again. "Sometimes, the man who stayed with the lady was there."

*The man who stayed with the lady.* Likely Daisy's husband since he was still alive then.

"But sometimes," Addie said, her voice small now, "there were other men. They didn't come when the lady was there. Only when she was gone."

"Did you know them?" the doctor asked.

Addie frantically shook her head and pulled her hands in a tight pose against her chest. "They were scary. They had guns."

All right. That hit Weston like a punch to the gut, and it darn sure didn't help when Addie's mouth started to tremble. "I don't like those men. They yell at the lady's man."

And Addie started to cry.

Not an ordinary cry. Sobs of a terrified little girl. It cut Weston to the core, and if Jericho hadn't caught onto him, he might have bolted forward to pull her into his arms. Weston soon realized, however, that Jericho had likely grabbed him to stop himself from doing the same thing.

"Did those men hurt you?" the doctor pressed.

"No. Just scary."

The relief hit Weston almost as hard as the anger. He hated that Addie had been through this, but he also knew it could have been a heck of a lot worse.

"I don't want to think about them anymore," Addie murmured.

"Okay. Then, let's talk about the other man, the one that brought you to the lady. Was he nice to you?"

Addie lifted her shoulder. "He gave me a donut. With sprinkles."

"Do you remember anything else about him? Like maybe his name? Or what he looked like?"

Another shake of her head. "No. Don't remember. I don't want to be here anymore. I want to go home." The sobs returned. "Please, let me go home. *Please.*"

The doctor looked back at them, not exactly asking permission to stop the session, because that's exactly what she did a few seconds later.

The moment Addie opened her eyes, her gaze went straight to Weston. And he went straight to her. He didn't even attempt to comfort her with words. Because there weren't any that'd help. But getting her out of there just might.

"I remember everything I said," she whispered to him.

A good lawman would have pressed to learn if there was something else. Something she hadn't talked about remembering. But Weston decided this wasn't the time to be a good lawman.

"Let's get her back to the safe house," he told Jericho, and her brother certainly didn't argue with that.

Since she didn't look too steady on her feet, Weston put the Kevlar vest back on her and scooped her up in his arms. There was no need to tell Jericho they were moving fast once they were outside. Jericho knew the possible dangers out there as well as Weston did.

"I'm okay, really," Addie said, not convincing him in the least.

Weston put her in the backseat of the marshals' car. Jericho, the doctor and the deputy followed along behind them as they drove away from the house and back onto the road. Eventually, when they were sure it was safe, Jericho would head back to the sheriff's office so that the doctor could write up her report. Addie, Weston and the marshals would spend yet another night in the safe house.

Addie looked up at Weston. "I didn't give you or the FBI anything you can use to find the killer."

"Not true. Thanks to you, we know several other men visited Daisy's house. We can question everyone in the area to see if they remember them."

Yes, it was a long shot, but that was true of this entire investigation.

"I kept thinking there was something else," she continued. "Something right at the edge of my memory."

"It might come to you." And if it did, Weston hoped like the devil that it didn't make her cry.

"Hell," Daniel snapped.

Weston looked up, following Daniel's gaze. There, ahead of them was a herd of cows ambling across the road. It wasn't that rare of a sight in rural Texas, but there was something about it that put Weston on full alert.

He soon figured out what.

When there was a break in the herd, he got a

glimpse of a car on the other side of the cows. A black limo.

One that Weston instantly recognized.

*Hell.*

IT TOOK ADDIE a moment to realize why Daniel had cursed. And why Weston had drawn his gun.

Canales and Boggs. Again.

This couldn't be a coincidence, and she was certain it was their limo since she'd caught a glimpse of the front license plate with the *AGB*.

"Get down," Weston told her, and he made sure she did just that by pushing her onto the seat.

The fear came, churning and twisting inside her. So did the anger. She was so tired of feeling this way.

"You see anything?" Weston asked the marshals.

"Just the limo and the cows," Daniel grumbled. "No one's getting out of the limo."

Addie could no longer see the limo. Just the cows that were meandering past the marshals' car. The cows were taking their time even though Kirk was honking the horn at them. Because of the noise from that and the cows themselves, it took her a moment to hear another sound.

One she definitely didn't want to hear.

A gunshot.

Addie wasn't sure where the bullet landed, but

it caused Weston to push her even farther down on the seat.

"The windows are bullet resistant," Daniel reminded them. "But I don't want to test that. Put the car in Reverse," he told Kirk, and he motioned out the back window, no doubt at Jericho.

Because of her position on the seat, she couldn't see Jericho's cruiser behind them, but Addie heard the squeal of the tires. Her brother was no doubt doing the same thing, trying to get the heck out of there.

"Hell," Kirk spat out. "An SUV just came up behind Jericho, and it's blocking the road."

And that meant they were trapped.

More shots came.

This time, Addie had no trouble figuring out where they landed because they smashed into the window right next to where Weston was seated.

Oh, mercy.

Someone was trying to kill them again. And it wasn't just a few shots. The barrage came, one bullet after another until the sound was deafening, and the windows on the right side of the car were webbed with the direct hits.

She tried to pull Weston down with her, but he stayed put, his gaze firing all around them. He couldn't lower what was left of the window to return fire, but if the shooters kept up, they'd have to figure out a way to return fire.

"You see the shooter?" Daniel asked.

"No," Kirk and Weston answered in unison. "The shots are coming from both sides."

That stopped her breath for a moment.

Addie wasn't familiar with this part of the county, but she remembered there were a lot of patches of thick trees and underbrush along the country road. Not many houses, either. Gunmen could have taken up position in those trees and then used the cows to stop them so they'd be easier targets.

And they'd succeeded.

"They're shooting at the limo, too," Kirk volunteered. "Their windows aren't stopping the bullets. And there's an SUV behind them as well, pinning them in."

Addie certainly hadn't expected that. Did it mean that Canales and Boggs weren't behind this attack? If they were, they were taking a huge chance with all those shots being fired.

"Can you see who's in the limo?" Weston asked him.

"No," Kirk readily answered.

So, maybe it wasn't Boggs and Canales inside, after all. But if they weren't there, then who was?

Behind them, Addie heard a horrible crash, the sound of metal ripping into metal. "Jericho," she said on a rise of breath.

Had he been hurt?

Addie lifted her head and managed to get a glimpse of her brother's cruiser crashing into the SUV that'd trapped them. But only a glimpse before Weston cursed and pushed her right back down.

"Don't get up again," Weston ordered her. He moved sideways in the seat, his attention volleying between the front and rear of the car. "Jericho's using his cruiser as a battering ram to get the SUV out of the way."

Addie wasn't sure if that would work. Or if it was the safe thing to do. But at this point, nothing was safe.

And it got worse.

She heard the shift in the direction of the gunfire. The shots no longer seemed to be aimed at the limo but rather at Jericho's cruiser. Whoever was out there had now made her brother a target.

"Hold on," Kirk warned them a split second before he gunned the engine.

Kirk didn't go straight ahead, however. He jerked the steering wheel to the right, and that's when Addie realized he was darting around what remained of the herd of cows still on the road. There had finally been a big enough opening for them to try to escape.

Good thing, too, because the bullets were coming even faster.

Almost immediately, Kirk jerked the car to the

right. No doubt so that he wouldn't crash right into the limo.

"My brother," she said. "We can't leave him here."

"Jericho's right behind us," Weston told her.

Addie believed him, but she lifted her head just a fraction to make sure Jericho was okay. She tried to take in everything at once.

Jericho's cruiser was there.

Just as Weston had said, it was behind them, weaving around the handful of cows still on the road. The limo was on the move, too, but it wasn't coming after them. It was speeding away in the opposite direction.

And then Addie saw something else.

A blur of motion at first.

A man.

And even though Weston tried to push her back down, Addie stayed put and motioned toward the person who was ducking behind one of the trees. The man didn't duck nearly fast enough, though, because Addie got a good look at his face.

Oh, God.

What was *he* doing there?

# *Chapter Sixteen*

Ogden.

Weston didn't like that the man kept turning up in bad situations. Like the latest attack near Daisy's house.

But Ogden had been there all right.

Weston had managed to get only a glimpse of him, but there was no mistaking that it was Ogden.

"Any luck finding Ogden?" Addie asked him.

Weston had to shake his head. For the past two hours, while the marshals were making their way back to the safe house, he'd been on the phone, trying to locate the man. But no one knew where he was. Jericho had sent several deputies to comb the woods near the attack, and they hadn't had any better luck finding him than Weston had.

"What about Canales and Boggs?" she pressed. "Anything else on them?"

She already knew parts of their update, that one

of the deputies had found Canales and Boggs. Or rather just Canales and his driver.

"We verified that Boggs wasn't within fifty miles of the attack," Weston explained. "He was at a fund-raiser. That doesn't make him innocent," he quickly added. "Because Boggs could have hired someone to fire those shots."

That someone could have been Ogden.

Though Weston had to admit he hadn't seen a gun in Ogden's hand, and since those shots had come from a rifle, a weapon of that size would have been hard to miss. Of course, Ogden could have discarded the gun when he realized his targets were getting away.

And one of those targets appeared to be Canales.

*Appeared* being the key word. Canales had escaped without so much as a scratch, so maybe he only wanted them to think he'd been in danger.

When Kirk took the final turn to the safe house, Daniel and Weston glanced around to make sure no one was following them. No one was. They had the road to themselves, just as they had for the bulk of the drive away from that nightmare of an attack. Eventually, they'd have to do reports and such, but for now Weston just wanted Addie off the road and someplace safe.

"Jericho hasn't had a chance to fully question Canales yet," Weston continued, talking to her.

"But Canales claims he was out there because he got a phone call from Ogden asking him to meet him."

"And he went?" There was plenty of skepticism in her voice. Weston felt the same way.

"Canales says that Ogden was threatening to derail the campaign by claiming to have proof that Boggs is the Moonlight Strangler. Canales said he wanted to get that so-called proof from Ogden."

"Yes, I'll bet he did. If the proof exists." She paused. "You think maybe Ogden managed to get a DNA sample from Boggs?"

"It's possible." Anything was at this point, but if Ogden did indeed have proof that Boggs was the Moonlight Strangler, then Ogden had a huge target on him. No way would Boggs let him live.

From the front seat, Daniel finished his latest call and turned to look back at them. "We found the owner of those cows. A small-time rancher not far from the road. Someone tore down his fence and herded the cows out of there. The guy doesn't have a record, or a connection to any of our suspects."

So it was another dead end.

Kirk pulled to a stop in front of the safe house, and Daniel got them inside while Kirk put the car in the detached garage. Probably so that the vehicle wouldn't be out in the open. The place was in the middle of the sticks, but if someone happened to drive by, those shot-out windows might cause them to get suspicious. Soon, the marshals would have to swap out vehicles, but since it was nearly sunset, that probably wouldn't happen until morning.

"You should try to eat something," Weston reminded Addie once they were inside.

"Maybe later. I need to catch my breath first," Addie added and headed for her bedroom.

Weston didn't get overly concerned until she shut the door. Oh, man. She was probably on the verge of a meltdown.

"You think she's okay?" Daniel asked while he set the security system.

"Probably not." Weston went after her. He gave one knock on the door before he opened it.

And his jaw dropped to the floor.

She sure wasn't falling apart but rather undressing. Addie already had her jeans unzipped and off her hips.

"They're too tight," she said, slipping them all the way off. Her short top gave him a nice view of her panties. Blue with little flowers. "It was making me queasy."

He doubted that was the only thing making her queasy. Unlike him. He suddenly felt a lot of things, but queasy wasn't on the list. Seeing Addie half-naked gave him all sorts of bad ideas.

And memories.

After all, they'd had a steamy kissing session in this very room the day before. A session his body reminded him of right now.

She glanced out into the hall. No marshals nearby but Weston closed it just in case they came by and got a glimpse of Addie searching for something to wear in the bag she'd packed. She finally pulled out a pair of gray flannel pajama bottoms. Hardly hot. Well, on anyone else, they wouldn't be.

But this was Addie.

With those curves, she could make a brown paper bag look hot.

"You're staring at me," she pointed out.

"Yeah," he admitted. "I'm trying to convince myself that it'd be a good idea to go in another room. Away from you. Away from the memory of just seeing you nearly naked."

Her eyebrow rose. "And?"

"I'm failing."

Addie managed a very short-lived smile. "I do a lot of failing when it comes to you."

Weston didn't like the sound of that. "What do you mean?"

"I didn't remember what needed to be remembered while I was with the therapist."

Hell. Not that. "Well, it might help if I could stop people from shooting at you. Nearly dying every day can put a damper on lots of things—memory included."

"Some memories," she whispered.

And just like that, they weren't talking about the hypnosis anymore. At least he didn't think they were. Addie wasn't falling apart as he'd predicted, but she was obviously beating herself up over something that wasn't her fault.

Addie took a deep breath, sank down on the foot of the bed. "What did you think the first time you saw me?"

All right. That didn't clear up much for him. Weston had never considered himself a pro at figuring out a woman's mind, but this was more confusing than usual.

"And it's okay to lie," she quickly added. "I'd rather not hear that you saw me and your first thought was 'she'll be good bait for a killer.'"

Weston wasn't confused at all about this answer. "That wasn't my first thought. And that isn't a lie. Truth is, when I first saw you, it was pure attraction."

But that was a partial lie. It didn't tell the whole story.

"I felt as if I'd been hit with a sack of bricks. *Good* bricks," he clarified. Though it hadn't exactly felt good at the time. "You were so beautiful that I had to remind myself to breathe."

Tears watered her eyes. The little smile returned. "Now, that's romantic."

"I'm not sure it was all romance I was feeling. Parts of me were just thinking sex. Well, one part of me anyway."

"That's okay." She stood, rubbing her hands on the sides of the pajama bottoms. "Parts of me were thinking the same thing about you."

"Really?" That gave him another hit of the fiery hot heat that he needed to start cooling down. "You were sort of an emotional mess. I figured sex was the last thing on your mind."

"Not sort of. I *was* an emotional mess. But seeing you seemed to cut right through all of that. The first time you kissed me, I could have sworn everything stopped. My heart. Any thoughts in my head."

Yeah. For him, it'd been like more bricks. Bad ones, that time. Because he'd known she was the only woman he'd ever want to kiss again.

Not exactly a comforting thought for a lawman living a lie.

She blinked away the tears, and her chin came up. He could see her steeling up for the next set of memories. The post-sex ones where he'd crushed her into a million little pieces.

What she didn't know was that he'd crushed himself, too.

"Will you ever forgive me?" he asked.

She didn't answer him. Not right away. "I'll forgive you if you'll give me something."

Before he jumped to say anything, Weston tried to think this through. "What do you want?"

Addie came to him. Put her arms around him. First one, then the other. "I need you to help me forget. Even if it's for a few minutes, I just need this noise in my head to stop."

Well, it wasn't a big declaration of feelings. Something Weston wasn't sure he wanted anyway.

"So…you want sex?' he clarified.

She shook her head. Kissed him. "I want sex *with you.* You're the only one who can get me through this."

Flattering, yes. Could he do it?

Oh, yeah.

But that nagging feeling in the back of his head shouted out one big question. Was this the right thing to do for Addie?

"If it's too much to ask…" she started.

"Sex with you isn't a chore," Weston interrupted. "But I want to make sure something else won't work just as well. Something that won't mess with your mind afterward."

She closed her eyes a moment, and when she opened them, he saw pretty much all he needed to see. The need. It went bone-deep in her.

"I don't want anyone or anything else," she

whispered. "Just you. Right here, right now. We'll deal with any mind-messing later."

Addie stared at him, clearly waiting.

"Did I convince you?" she asked.

Hearing one of his favorite lines aimed at him nearly made him smile. Nearly. However, it was hard to smile when her body brushed against his.

Weston took that as the move of a woman who was certain of what she wanted. And yes, it convinced him.

He didn't deserve, but he'd take it. Not just the kiss, either. He took her. Into his arms, pulling her close to him.

His body instantly geared up for sex. And he knew it'd be good. But gearing up for sex was just the start. There was no way he could get Addie into bed again and not have it change their lives forever.

The question was—*how* would it change things?

Weston mentally repeated that, tried to come up with the consequences, but those thoughts flew right out of his head when he deepened the kiss.

This was wrong on so many levels. The danger breathing down their necks. The emotional complications from the pregnancy. Addie should be resting, but judging from the way she was kissing him, there'd be no rest for either of them.

Part of him wanted to stop, but there wasn't

much common sense left for him. Just more of that feeling he'd just been hit with more bricks.

"Three months is long time to go without you," she whispered, her breath hitting his mouth. "And I don't count the third base yesterday."

That was enough of a green light. Of course, with his erection testing the limits of his boxers, almost anything she would have said to him—other than stop—would have been a green light.

Well, she wasn't saying stop.

And Weston didn't, either.

He caught onto her top and slipped it off her so he could kiss the tops of her breasts. She helped with that, too, by unhooking her bra so he could taste her the way he wanted. She was warm, her skin like silk but she tasted like something forbidden.

Which she was in some ways.

That's probably why it only fired them hotter, and it didn't take many of those breast kisses before Weston wanted a whole lot more. Addie clearly wanted more, too, because the battle started to get them each undressed.

He had the easy part, and while Addie was still grabbling with his shirt, Weston reached over and locked the door. In the same motion, he pulled off her pajama bottoms and her panties. In just a couple of moves, he had her naked and back on the bed. Where he kissed her.

On her stomach.

And lower.

He really liked going lower, and the kiss must have been right where Addie wanted it because she froze. For a couple of seconds. Then she made that sound. That moan of pleasure that went through every inch of him.

"No. You're not finishing things that way," she insisted, latching onto his hair. "No third base this time."

Well, that only left one thing, and Addie was working hard to make sure that happened. She hauled him away from the *lower* kisses, all the while battling with his jeans. Since she just wasn't very good at the whole undressing-a-man thing, Weston helped her. He managed to get all the necessary clothes kicked or pulled off. He'd have bruises, but they'd be worth it.

Their bodies were in a frenzy by the time Weston made it back up to her mouth, and even though that brainless part of him was pushing him to take her now, he took a moment just to look at her.

Oh, man.

Would he ever be able to see her like this and not feel as if someone had sucked all the air from the room? He hoped not.

"Homerun time," she murmured.

It was. And it darn nearly felt like a homerun

when he pushed inside her. That kick was more of a punch from a heavyweight's fist now, and it took him a moment to rein himself in enough to find the rhythm Addie needed.

Not that she needed much.

Maybe because of the three months without, or maybe the adrenaline and nerves was playing into this. Either way, it didn't last nearly long enough. Addie slipped her legs around him. Her arms, too.

And she flew into a million little pieces.

"Do this with me," she begged.

That was the plan.

Again, it didn't take much of an effort. Addie had done the hard part by taking him to the brink, and Weston let her climax finish him off.

## *Chapter Seventeen*

Addie woke up in Weston's arms.

He was naked. So was she. And she had settled against him as if she belonged there. Even more, she'd actually slept, something she hadn't managed to do for a while. Not since the attacks had started.

Apparently, Weston had a cure for insomnia.

A cure for a lot of other things, too, since now even hours later, she could still feel the slack pleasure sliding through her. Of course, that pleasure was already starting to slip away as the questions came. Well, one big question anyway.

What was next?

In just six short months they'd be parents. Forever bonded by the child they'd created. But that didn't mean that bond would extend to more of this.

Addie glanced at his bare chest and got another dose of the heat that only Weston could dole out.

If they stayed around each other, there'd definitely be *more of this.*

And that's why she had to be careful.

Sex could cloud things, especially her judgment, and she didn't want to jump into a relationship with Weston until she was sure that was what he wanted.

"Go back to sleep," he whispered. He never even opened his eyes but idly brushed a kiss on her forehead, pulled her closer to him.

"Do I snore?" she asked. "Is that how you knew I was awake?"

Probably not the best question after sex, but it bothered her that he could tell without even looking at her that she hadn't been sleeping.

He laughed. A low and smoky sound that fanned more of those flames inside her. Of course, anything at this point would have fanned her flames.

"No snoring. The rhythm of your breathing changed."

She thought about that for a second. "You were tuned in to that?"

He lifted one eyelid, peeked out at her. "I'm tuned in to a lot of things when it comes to you."

Mercy, the man knew just what to say to turn her to mush. And to make her even more confused.

"Want to talk about it?" he asked. Apparently, he also had the tune-in ability to read her mind.

Addie didn't want to talk about it, not until she'd sorted out her feelings for him. That might take a while. She didn't even get a chance to tell him that, though, because his phone buzzed.

She groaned, checked the time. It was only ten o'clock at night, but she figured anyone calling now wouldn't be delivering good news.

Weston groaned, too, and maneuvered himself to a sitting position so he could grab his phone from the nightstand. He groaned again when he saw the name on the screen.

"Boggs, what the hell do you want?" Weston snapped when he answered the call. He put it on speaker, but Addie was so close she would have had no trouble hearing whatever the man had to say.

"We need to talk," Boggs insisted. "*Now.* I have something to tell Addie. And it's important."

All right. That got her attention, and Addie sat up, as well. Weston seemed more riled than curious. Probably because he knew they couldn't trust anything Boggs had to say.

"What do you need to tell her?" Weston demanded.

"I'll only say it to Addie and you face-to-face."

Of course Boggs would want something like that. Since he was a top suspect not just for the attacks but also for being the Moonlight Strangler, Addie didn't want to get anywhere near him unless he was behind bars.

"Is this a joke?" Weston cursed. "It has to be because you know a meeting with Addie isn't going to happen."

"It has to happen." Now it was Boggs who groaned, but it didn't sound like it was out of frustration. Was he upset about something? Maybe over the fact they were close to catching him?

"If it has to happen," Weston continued, "then it'll happen over the phone. If you've got something to say to Addie, then start talking."

But Boggs didn't do that. He hesitated. A long time. "It's too late. Everything has been set in motion."

Weston looked at her, no doubt to see if she knew what he was talking about, but Addie had to shake her head. Still, this sounded like the start of an admission of some kind of guilt. Weston must have thought so, too, because he hit the function on his phone to record the conversation.

"What the hell are you talking about?" Weston pressed when Boggs didn't continue.

"I'm talking about Addie. And those memories she had from childhood."

That rid her of any remnants of the heat she'd been feeling just minutes earlier. "What memories?" she asked.

Weston frowned at her, probably because he

hadn't wanted her to be part of this conversation. But Addie was part of it. Heck, she was the reason for it, and Boggs might say more to her than he would to Weston.

"What memories?" she repeated when Boggs gave them the silent treatment again.

"You tell me." Boggs no longer sounded upset. The anger crept into his voice. "The FBI is scrambling to listen to the recording of your session from earlier today, the one you did at Daisy's house. And I can't get a single person to tell me what's on those recordings."

Good grief. That's what this is about? But Addie rethought that. Maybe this meant Boggs believed she'd remembered exactly who he was.

Her birth father and a serial killer.

"You expect us to be torn up that you don't have a rat in the FBI who'll leak secrets to you?" Weston challenged. "Or is this some kind of confession? If so, spit it out."

"No confession. Not about that anyway. I just know that childhood memories can be planted." Boggs paused again. "And I think that's exactly what happened with Addie."

Since she hadn't remembered much, Addie doubted the planted-memory theory. If someone had gone to the trouble to do that, they would have planted details that would have led to her identifying something or someone. But it did lead her to another question.

"Do you really think someone would have tried to plant memories about you?" she asked.

"Of course." No hesitation that time. "I'm a powerful man in the middle of a campaign, and what better way to discredit me than to try to smear my name with the false memories planted in your head."

"Who would have done that?" Weston snapped.

"I'm not sure."

But Addie got the feeling that Boggs did know. Was he trying to protect Ogden because he was Boggs's own son? Or was this about his old friend, Canales?

"You know," Weston continued, "there's one way for you to discredit what Addie remembered. You could have a DNA test done to prove you're not the Moonlight Strangler."

"What did she remember?" Boggs shouted.

So Weston had hit a big nerve with the hint, or rather the lie, that she'd witnessed something as a child, something to indicate that Boggs was indeed the serial killer.

"I'll tell you what she remembered when I have your DNA results," Weston countered.

"No." Boggs shouted that, too. And he repeated it. "I'm not the Moonlight Strangler. I'm not!"

"Then prove it." Weston put that challenge out there. And they waited. And waited.

"A DNA test could be a problem for me," Boggs finally said. "Not because it would prove I'm a killer. It wouldn't. But I have a secret that needs to stay hidden."

"Excuse me?" Weston cursed again. "This is a murder investigation, Boggs. You're a suspect, and that's about to be all over the news. So what secret is worse than that?"

"I fathered a child." Boggs sounded as if he were choosing his words carefully. "Not Addie."

"Ogden?" Addie asked.

"No. Not him, either. A son who was born twenty years ago. A lowlife. And his DNA's in the system because of multiple arrests. He has nothing to do with the Moonlight Strangler, nothing to do with the attacks or your investigation."

It didn't take Addie long to fill in the blanks. "But if people found out that you fathered this *lowlife* while cheating on your wife, it wouldn't mesh with the family values you're spouting about in your campaign."

Boggs's silence confirmed that. However, that wasn't the only question Addie had.

"'It's too late,' you said earlier. 'Everything has been set into motion.' What did you mean?"

Yet another long hesitation. "I'm sorry, Addie. Really sorry."

Boggs ended the call, and, still cursing, Weston hit redial. The man didn't answer, but there was a knock at the bedroom door. Addie was still reeling from Boggs's call so it took her a moment to realize something had to be wrong for one of the marshals to come to her door at night.

"You need to get up right now," Daniel said from the other side of the door.

Weston did, and while he pulled on his boxers, he hurried to throw open the door. "What happened?"

"Our location's been compromised," Daniel said, already hurrying back up the hall. "We need to move Addie right now."

WESTON FOUGHT THROUGH that punch of dread and began to throw on his clothes. Addie did the same.

One glance at her and, even in the dim light, he could see the fear on her face. He hated that it was there. Hated that once again they might be on the verge of another attack.

"Compromised? How?" Weston called out to Daniel.

"We're not sure yet. But someone just triggered the sensor on the road."

"Maybe a deer or something?" Weston hoped. Prayed, actually. Anything was better than another hired gun. Or worse—the Moonlight Strangler.

"No," Daniel answered. "It's someone in a car."

Hell. Weston doubted this was someone out for an evening drive.

"Maybe it's nothing," she whispered.

"Maybe." But Weston figured Addie didn't believe that any more than he did.

He finished dressing, fast, and with Addie right behind him, they went into the hall. The lights had already all been turned off, and Kirk was at the front window, his gun drawn and a pair of night scope binoculars pressed to his eyes.

"See anything?" Weston asked. Beside him, Daniel slipped on a Kevlar vest and handed one to Weston and another to Addie. Kirk was already wearing one.

"I'm not seeing nearly enough." Kirk handed the binoculars to Weston so he could have a look. Before he did, however, Weston motioned for Addie to stay away from the windows.

It took Weston a moment to spot the dark-colored SUV. It wasn't moving but it was parked about thirty yards from the house. He couldn't see the driver through the tinted windshield, but the exhaust from the engine was mixing with the cold air and was creating a mist around the vehicle.

"I've already called for backup," Daniel explained, "but we're looking at thirty minutes or more before it arrives."

That was way too long. Weston doubted whoever was in that SUV would wait a half hour before doing whatever he was planning on doing. But it did make him wonder—why was the driver just sitting there? Maybe because whoever arrived for backup would be walking into a trap.

"I'm going out the back door," Kirk said, already heading to the door off the kitchen. "I need to check the car and see if someone managed to put a tracking device on it."

Well, that would explain how the place had been compromised, since Weston was certain they hadn't been followed. However, it wouldn't explain how someone had managed to put a tracker on the car in the first place.

Unless…

Weston cursed. "Someone could have been hiding in the ditch during that last attack."

With all the chaos going on—the cows and the shots being fired—they wouldn't have easily noticed something like that. Especially since the side windows had been cracked and webbed from the bullets.

Daniel made a sound of agreement and hurried to the side window. No doubt so he could cover Kirk. The detached garage wasn't far, only about five feet from the house, but Kirk would be out in the open for a few critical moments where he could be gunned down.

"Get on the floor behind the sofa," Weston told Addie, and he kept his attention on the SUV.

The vehicle still wasn't moving. It was just sitting there like a dangerous animal stalking them.

There was a swooshing sound. Not a gunshot, though. A moment later, Daniel cursed and ran toward the back door.

Weston saw it then. The blaze in the garage. Someone had launched a firebomb into the building.

"What's wrong?" Addie asked.

Weston wanted to assure her that everything was okay, but it wasn't. Far from it. "Did Kirk get out?" Weston called to Daniel.

A moment later, though, he had his answer when Kirk practically came crashing through the back door. "We need to get out of the house," Kirk insisted, his words rushed. His breath gusting.

Addie's was gusting, too, and even though she couldn't see the fire in the garage, she could no doubt smell the smoke that was already starting to make its way to the house.

"Who's out there?" Weston asked.

But Kirk shook his head and motioned for them to hurry to the door. "Someone with darn good aim—on the road near that SUV. The car's destroyed, and I'm thinking the house will be the next target."

It would be.

That meant they had to get out now. No choice about that. But it also meant that person with *darn good aim* could pick them off the moment they stepped outside.

Weston grabbed a coat from the sofa and handed it to Addie. In the same motion, he took hold of her arm and got her moving.

When they'd arrived at the safe house, he'd familiarized himself with the grounds, and there wasn't much out there they could use for cover. Still, there were a few things that might work especially since it was dark.

*Might.*

They headed for a woodpile about three feet high on the side of the house, and they ducked behind it while Addie put on the coat. It was freezing, literally, but they might not have a choice about being outside until backup arrived. Maybe the coat would help. Maybe the Kevlar vest would, too, though Kevlar wouldn't stop a fatal bullet to the head.

Weston positioned Addie between himself and the woodpile so he could give her at least some protection. His gaze fired all around them. The marshals did the same. And Weston got his first real look at the garage.

Or rather what was left of it.

The fire was already eating its way through the wooden building, and soon it would be nothing but ash. But why had their attackers gone after the car instead of the house?

Obviously, the person behind this hadn't wanted them to use the car to escape, but if that firebomb had gone into the house, then they probably wouldn't have been in any shape to get out of there. And it was possible they'd all be dead.

Did that mean the person didn't want to kill them?

That question was still repeating in his head when he heard another of those swishing sounds. Weston pushed Addie to the ground.

Just in time.

Judging from the sound of breaking glass, the firebomb crashed through one of the windows in the front of the house, and within seconds, the flames and the smoke started to shoot out.

"The idiot who fired that is somewhere on the road near the car," Daniel told them.

Yeah, Weston had already come to the same conclusion. He'd come to another conclusion, too.

A bad one.

If the shooter could launch a firebomb at the house and the garage, then he could also hit the woodpile.

"We need to warn the backup," Weston insisted. "And we need to move."

Kirk took care of a text to warn whoever was responding as backup so Weston glanced around for a possible escape route. They didn't exactly have a lot of options, though. Basically, everything in the line of sight of the shooter was off-limits.

That left the old barn.

And it was a good thirty yards away.

Thankfully, the darkness, fire and the smoke had created a semicover that would hopefully conceal them enough, and the barn was probably out of range from their attacker. If the guy tried to get closer to deliver a firebomb into the barn, then he'd face the same problem they had.

Very little cover.

Weston would be able to see him and maybe take him out.

"Are you thinking what I'm thinking?" Daniel asked him, tipping his head to the barn.

Weston nodded. There were two trees between the barn and them and an old bathtub that'd likely been used as a watering trough. It's wasn't much but it'd have to do.

"Stay low and move fast," Weston told Addie, and helped her to her feet.

The marshals took up cover on either side of her while Weston stayed in front. They started to run the moment they came out from behind the woodpile and headed for the tub.

Not a second too soon.

Because the third firebomb came flying through the air.

# *Chapter Eighteen*

Addie didn't look back, but she heard the now-familiar sound of the firebomb crashing into something. The woodpile, no doubt, and she had that confirmed when the four of them scrambled behind the old cast-iron tub.

Sweet heaven.

If they'd stayed just another second or two, they would have been caught in that tinderbox. Her heart was already in her throat. Already pounding too hard. She tried to steady it for the baby's sake, but she failed.

The ground was frozen, and it didn't take long for the cold to seep through her jeans and shoes. Weston was practically on top of her, the front of his body pressing against her back. She could feel the thud of his heartbeat and the tightness of his muscles.

"It'll be okay," Weston told her.

At best that was wishful thinking, but Addie figured it was closer to a lie than anything else.

They were far from okay, and if backup didn't arrive soon, they could all die.

Because the Moonlight Strangler or someone else wanted to kill her.

That broke her heart, not only for her precious baby. But also for Weston and the marshals who'd gotten caught up in this mess.

Addie looked back, and her gaze connected with Weston's. Thanks to the watery moonlight, she could actually see him. Despite his attempt to reassure her, the worry and the fear were right there, all over his face. But she also saw something else.

Determination.

"He's not getting to you," Weston said like an oath.

Even though there was no way he could guarantee that, it gave her hope and was a reminder that she couldn't give in to the fear. The stakes were too high for that.

"We have to move fast again," Weston added a moment later.

She'd already spotted the pair of trees between them and the barn, and that's where they headed. Addie held her breath, bracing herself for another firebomb or even gunfire.

But nothing happened.

They made it to the trees, ducking behind them. Immediately, the marshals and Weston surveyed the area. No doubt looking for anyone trying to sneak closer. But it was impossible to see the road now because of the smoke and fire.

"Come on," Daniel said, and they all took off again.

Even though Weston was keeping watch, he was also glancing at her. And cursing. Probably because he was afraid that all of this running wouldn't be good for the baby. That didn't concern her so much since she'd been physically active on the ranch, but Addie was terrified about what the stress was doing. And that thought brought on the anger.

She hated that monster out there. Hated that he was trying to take everything away from her.

They moved behind another tree. Not nearly wide enough to cover them all, and that's likely why they only stayed there a few seconds. Just long enough for Addie to catch her breath.

They started for the barn. Such as it was. It appeared to be falling apart, and the door was literally hanging on by a hinge. It was swaying back and forth with the gusting night air.

Her lungs were burning now from the cold and exertion. And she was shivering despite the jacket. Every step they took was a reminder that it could be her last.

But no more firebombs.

No shots of any kind.

They finally made it to the rickety barn, and Weston pulled her behind the back of it. There was no door there, only the one in the front, but he soon took care of that problem. He bashed his shoulder against some of the boards. It didn't take much for several of them to give way, and he pushed them aside to make an opening.

"Wait here," Daniel insisted, and he stooped down to maneuver himself through the makeshift opening.

Daniel kept his gun lifted, but he didn't go far. Just a few steps inside. "Can't see a thing," he grumbled.

Too bad. Because someone could be hiding in there. Yes, there was a sensor on the road, but that didn't mean their attacker hadn't managed to get a hired thug in through the pasture and into the barn.

Daniel moved deeper into the barn while the rest of them waited. Addie forced herself to slow down her breathing and tried to stay calm. Hard to do with every nerve in her body on full alert.

That full alert went even higher when she heard a sound. Not from inside the barn but from the area in front of the burning house.

A gunshot.

And it came right at them.

Weston cursed, sheltering her with his body.

Or at least he was trying to do that. The shooter clearly had them in his line of sight.

"Get inside," Weston insisted, and he pushed her through the opening of the barn, following right in behind her.

Kirk stepped in as well, the three lawmen instantly pivoting in all directions. No doubt looking for anyone who was about to attack them.

The barn was indeed dark, but there was some moonlight filtering in through the front door. There were also holes in the roof, and the light came through like needles hitting on the hay-strewn floor. Not nearly enough illumination, though, to see much beyond where they were standing in the middle of the barn.

There were shadows.

Plenty of them. And plenty of places for a gunman to hide, too.

It was also cold. So cold that Addie could see her own breath, and she started to shiver.

None of them said a word. They all stood there, just listening. And thankfully the shots outside stopped so that made it a little easier to hear what was going on. Well, it would have if the wind hadn't been causing that door to creak or if her own heartbeat hadn't been crashing in her ears.

Weston maneuvered her away from the opening. Away from the door, too, and about five feet away into what was left of a stall. Daniel stayed in front of her while Kirk went to the left. Weston, to the right.

Both searching the area.

Both also keeping watch on the front door in case the shooter tried to make his way inside.

Her breath froze when Weston came to an abrupt stop, and he whipped his gun toward the far right front corner. Not too far from that creaking door.

Daniel was a big man, but Addie came up on her toes so she could see what had captured Weston's attention. And she soon saw it.

Something, or maybe some*one*, in the shadows.

"Get down!" Weston shouted, and he did the same, diving to the side of some crumbling hay bales.

At that moment, a gust of wind caught the barn door and slapped it fully open so that the shadow was no longer a shadow. It was a man, and Addie saw his face.

And she also saw the gun he held in his hand.

OGDEN.

Of course.

Weston figured Ogden had some part in this, and that gun in his hand proved he was up to his old tricks. He was there to try to kill Addie again, but Weston had no intention of letting him do that.

"Addie, stay down," Weston warned her, and he took aim at Ogden.

Weston expected the man to fire or at least try to duck behind something. But he didn't. Ogden just stood there, staring at him.

"Why are you here?" Ogden asked.

Not only was it a strange question, Ogden's body language was strange, too. He had his left hand bracketed on the barn wall, using it to support himself.

The barn door shut again, but Weston's eyes had adjusted enough to the darkness that he could see that Ogden wasn't pointing the gun at them. It was aimed at the floor.

"What are you doing here?" Weston fired back.

Ogden shook his head and looked around. Not the kind of look of a man trying to escape or decide what to do. He was looking at the place as if seeing it for the first time.

"Why did you bring me here?" Ogden said.

Weston cursed. Then he groaned. Either Ogden was high or drunk, or else he wanted to make it seem that way. It wouldn't matter which. Weston didn't trust this fool for a minute. Nor would he let Ogden distract him so that the hired guns could come in for the kill.

He motioned for Kirk to keep watch at the back. Weston did the same at the front, but he doubted he'd actually be able to see anyone sneaking up on them. The darkness would work in favor of their attackers, and there were plenty of ways to get to the barn. Of course, a shooter wouldn't have to get too close to send another firebomb their way.

"I didn't bring you here," Weston said to Ogden, "but you're going to tell me why you're holding that gun."

Ogden glanced at the gun then. And he dropped it. He frantically shook his head again. "That's not my gun." He touched his fingers to his temple. "Did you give me pills or something to get me here?"

"I didn't give you anything."

Weston went closer to Ogden to kick the gun out of his reach. He also patted the man down. Ogden wasn't carrying any other weapons. Nor did he smell of alcohol. However, he was wobbly, and if Weston hadn't helped Ogden lean against the wall, he probably would have fallen.

Heck, maybe someone had drugged him, or he could have drugged himself. Once backup arrived, Ogden could be taken and tested. Too bad backup was still probably fifteen minutes out.

"Now it's your turn to answer some questions," Weston demanded. "Did you hire those shooters out there?"

Ogden's eyes widened. "No. Why would I do something like that?"

"You tell me. But my guess is you wanted to

try to have another go at Addie. Especially since that attack on the road failed big-time."

"Attack?"

"Yeah, you know—the one where you blocked the road with the cows and then tried to kill Addie."

No headshaking this time. "That wasn't me."

"I saw you," Addie insisted. "You were in the woods near Daisy's house."

Ogden made a sound of disbelief. "But I wasn't there to kill you. I was running for my life."

Weston made his own sound. One of skepticism to let Ogden know he wasn't buying any of it. "And you just happened to be in the same area when bullets started flying?"

"Yes, because I escaped from a car. Someone kidnapped me again. Like this time. Someone must have kidnapped me and brought me here."

"Who would do that?"

Ogden didn't answer Weston for a long time, and the already distressed look on his face got a whole lot worse. "My father maybe."

"The Moonlight Strangler brought you here?" Weston was fishing for info and hoped he didn't get a yes from Ogden. Not on this anyway.

Ogden turned toward the stall where he'd heard Addie's voice. "Addie, you have to believe me. I don't want you dead. Not anymore. I was confused. I thought my father was telling me to kill you. But I don't think it was my father doing that."

"Then who was it?" Weston asked.

Ogden opened his mouth to answer, but the sound of the blast stopped him. Not from a firebomb this time but from another bullet. And this shot sounded a whole lot closer than the other ones.

Weston kept an eye on Ogden, but he pivoted in the direction of the barn door. Just as another shot came.

This one slammed into the rotting wood at the front of the barn. And it wasn't a single shot. More came. One right after another, and Weston had no choice but to dive back to the ground with Addie. He also heard something else he didn't want to hear.

A thud.

And Daniel started cursing.

Kirk had fallen and was clutching his chest.

Hell, the marshal had been shot.

Except he hadn't been, Weston quickly realized. No blood. The gunman had fired a shot into the Kevlar vest that Kirk was wearing. It wouldn't be deadly, but Weston knew from experience that it hurt like the devil, and it'd clearly knocked the breath from Kirk because he was gasping for air.

Gasping in pain, too.

Daniel pulled Kirk to the side, away from the

door, and began to unstrap the vest so he could get the scalding hot bullet off Kirk's skin.

The shots didn't stop. They continued to tear their way through the barn.

"Get down!" Weston yelled to Ogden when the man just stood there in a daze.

Ogden seemed to freeze. For a second or two. And then he got down all right.

But not the way Weston had figured he would.

Ogden, too, clutched his chest. No Kevlar vest for him. So, this time, there was indeed some blood.

He'd been shot.

"Help me," Ogden groaned before collapsing to the ground.

Weston didn't go to Ogden because he heard something behind him. Not Kirk or Daniel. But something else.

Something that got his complete attention.

Addie made a strangled sound.

And that's when Weston saw the man come through the back opening and put the gun to Addie's head.

## *Chapter Nineteen*

Addie didn't move fast enough. She'd heard the footsteps behind her a split second too late and hadn't scrambled out of the way in time.

It could turn out to be a deadly mistake.

Because someone now had her at gunpoint and was using her as a human shield to stop Weston and the marshals from shooting him.

The fear slammed through her, but she tried not to panic. Hard to do, though, when her baby was right back in danger again.

She couldn't see her attacker's face. But Weston could. And judging from his profanity and glare, he knew the man. So this probably wasn't just another hired gun but rather the person behind all these attacks.

"Canales," she said without having to look back at him.

Boggs wasn't much taller than she was, and this man was stooping, trying to keep his body hidden behind hers. It had to be Canales.

"Put down that gun and move away from Addie," Weston ordered him.

"You really think that'll work?" Canales asked, the sarcasm dripping from his voice. "I'll put it down when I'm done here. Which shouldn't be long. I just need a few answers."

"So do we," Weston fired back.

Daniel made a sound of agreement about that and moved protectively in front of Kirk, who was still on the ground trying to regain his breath.

"Is he dead?" Canales asked tipping his head to Ogden.

Weston didn't even look back at Ogden. He kept his attention focused on Canales and her. "Probably. Why, are you all torn up about that?"

"No. But he would have made such a good scapegoat. I'd planned on pinning all of this on him. Copycatting his daddy will make good press. The reporters will gobble it up."

They would. *If* Canales got away with this. Addie had to figure out a way to make sure he didn't.

"Now all of you toss your guns into the center of the barn," Canales demanded. "If you don't do it right now, I'll shoot Addie. I won't kill her yet, but I will hurt her."

She believed him, and any shot could cause her to miscarry. Still, it sickened her when the marshals and Weston threw their guns onto the floor near Canales. She wasn't sure if Weston had a backup weapon on him or not. They'd run from the house in such a hurry that it was possible none of them had another gun they could use to try to put a stop to this.

"I'm surprised you didn't send one of your hired lackeys to do your dirty work," Weston said to Canales.

"My *lackeys* have failed, time and time again. And because they didn't do their jobs, Addie got yet another round with that therapist." Canales put his mouth against her ear. "I just need to know what you remembered during the hypnosis session."

So that's what this was about. Or at least part of it. She knew from the DNA test that Canales wasn't the Moonlight Strangler, but it didn't mean he wasn't working for him.

"Is Boggs the Moonlight Strangler?" she asked.

"Answer my question!" Canales shouted.

She jumped from the sheer volume of his voice, but Addie steeled herself. Or rather tried to do that. "You answer mine first, and then I'll tell you what you want to know. Is Boggs the Moonlight Strangler?"

"Not a chance." Canales mumbled some raw profanity. "The man can barely tie his own shoes. Hardly the serial killer type. He's much better suited to being a politician. Or at least the front for a politician, and that was our arrangement."

It was possible Boggs could be lured into a deal like that. But did that mean Boggs was innocent? Or maybe he was in on this plan. If so, backup might be able to capture him if he was out there somewhere. Of course, her first hope was that backup would be able to save Weston, the marshals and her.

"So who's the Moonlight Strangler?" Weston snapped.

"Wouldn't have a clue," Canales answered, "but I'll soon find out. He's not pleased with me. I got some nasty letters telling me to back off. Or else. I went with the *or else* and decided to set a trap for him. If all went well, that trap is being sprung as we speak."

A trap? She wondered what it was. Or if Canales was even telling the truth. After all, he didn't need the Moonlight Strangler around if he wanted to pin their deaths on him and Ogden.

"You decided to let everyone believe the Moonlight Strangler was behind this," she concluded. And Canales sure didn't deny it.

"We're getting off track, and I don't have a lot of time." Canales jammed the gun even harder against Addie's head. "What did you remember?" he repeated.

Addie winced, hoping her sound of pain didn't send Weston charging at the man. He certainly looked ready to tear Canales limb from limb.

"I didn't remember anything," she said.

"Liar! The FBI's doing all kinds of checks on gunrunning operations in the area thirty years ago."

So, they were back to that. "I didn't remember any gunrunning, only men with guns."

"Tell me everything you said to that FBI shrink." Even though she still couldn't see his face, Addie knew he was speaking through clenched teeth.

Anything she said to him right now was a risk. A huge one. But there was no way he would allow any of them to live anyway. No. His plan was likely to learn whatever information she had and then he'd kill them all. Canales couldn't leave them as witnesses. After that, he'd work on trying to cover everything up.

"I remembered you." Addie let that hang between them for several moments. "Of course, I didn't know your name at the time, but I was able to describe the guns. And Boggs and you. The two of you came once when Daisy wasn't there. You met with her husband."

She held her breath, waiting and praying that her lie wouldn't get her killed right here, right now.

Addie had no idea if Canales had actually ever been to Daisy's house, much less with Boggs and a gun shipment. The only thing she had remembered were several armed men. She had no clear images of their faces.

But Canales didn't know that.

"You don't have to worry, though," she continued, "the statute of limitations is up on the gunrunning."

She left it at that, though Canales no doubt knew that the gunrunning was the least of his problems. The conspiracy. The cover-up. All of that would send him to jail for the rest of his life.

A feral sound tore from his throat. "Everything I've worked for could be gone. And all because of you!"

He dug the gun barrel so hard into her temple that she felt the skin break. Addie clamped her teeth over her bottom lip to stop herself from crying out in pain, but she hadn't needed Weston to hear anything for him to react. He charged toward Canales.

Canales reacted, too. Fast.

He turned the gun on Weston. And Canales fired.

The shot was deafening, and it drowned out Addie's own scream. Everything was one big blur of shouts and movement, but the only thing she could think of was Weston.

Mercy, had he been shot? Or worse. Was he dead?

It took her several painful moments to focus on what had actually happened. Weston had scrambled to the side of the barn, and even though she couldn't see all of him, he was alive. He lifted his head from behind one of the hay bales.

"Try that again," Canales warned him, "and I'll have the privilege of killing you myself. The same goes for you two," he added to the other marshals.

Her ears were roaring from the blast, and the shock of nearly losing Weston had put her in panic mode. But she finally heard something she'd wanted to hear since this latest nightmare had started.

Sirens.

Backup was finally here.

Of course, that didn't mean they were all safe. She was betting Canales had hired thugs stashed out there somewhere. Judging from the threat he'd just made, he planned on using those thugs to finish them off.

"This isn't over," Canales insisted. "I can do damage control with the FBI. And I can discredit the memories of a brat-kid, especially one with killer blood running through her veins."

As it usually did, the killer blood comment

turned her stomach. But from the corner of the barn, she heard a loud groan. Not one of pain, either.

It was the sound of outrage.

At first she thought it'd come from Weston. But then Addie saw Ogden come off the ground. He snatched up his gun.

And pulled the trigger.

WESTON CURSED HIMSELF.

He'd been so focused on stopping Canales that he hadn't noticed Ogden. Weston moved as fast as he could and prayed it was fast enough to stop a bullet from hitting Addie.

But it was already too late.

Except the shot hadn't gone toward Addie, Weston quickly realized.

Ogden had shot into the back opening of the barn. At first Weston thought the man just had bad aim, but then he heard someone groan. The ski-mask wearing gunman who'd been waiting outside crumpled to the ground. Weston hadn't had the right angle so he hadn't even known the guy was out there.

Canales cursed and moved, too, dragging Addie to the side of the barn.

Or rather that's what he was trying to do.

Addie wasn't making it easy for him. She was fighting to get away, and she rammed her elbow into the man's stomach. It didn't stop him, but Canales did bash his gun against the side of Addie's head.

The rage went through him, so strong that Weston could have sworn he saw red.

Weston grabbed his gun from the floor and raced toward Canales. The man still didn't have control of Addie, though he tried to put the gun to her head. Not that he would need a head shot to kill her. With all the struggling going on, the gun could accidentally go off, and he could lose both Addie and the baby.

He had to make sure that didn't happen.

Weston immediately tossed his gun aside so he could dive into the fray. He hit the ground, hard, and it nearly knocked the breath out of him. Still, that didn't stop him. Weston latched onto Canales's hand while he tried to push Addie out of the way.

From the corner of his eye, Weston saw Daniel run in Ogden's direction. Good. Yes, Ogden had shot that ski-mask-wearing thug, but there was no telling what else he would do.

Canales kicked Weston, the blow landing right in his stomach. It dazed him for a second. Just enough for Canales to grab Addie by the hair and drag her a few inches away.

Weston went after him again.

No way was he letting Canales hurt her. But

that's exactly what Canales was trying to do. Addie had hold of his right wrist and she was obviously trying to wrestle the gun away from him, but Canales was a lot stronger and bigger than she was, and he got the barrel aimed at her head again.

"Back off," Canales growled to Weston.

With Addie still struggling, Canales managed to get into the corner with her. Hell. She was his hostage again.

Outside, the sirens stopped, and Weston couldn't hear the sounds of anyone about to burst in and rescue them. It was entirely possible that Canales's hired guns had overpowered the backup, too.

"You want her to die?" Canales taunted. "Then, make a move toward me. She won't have time to draw another breath."

Weston believed him, and that's the only reason he didn't lunge at the man. For now anyway. But when he got the chance, he was going to make Canales pay, and pay hard, for this.

In the darkness, Weston's gaze met Addie's. She no longer looked terrified, and that wasn't a look of surrender in her eyes.

"I'm sorry," she said.

Weston shook his head. "Don't." He didn't know exactly what she had in mind, but he didn't want her trying to fight her way out of this. "Think of the baby," Weston added.

Yeah, it was dirty, but it worked. He saw that in her eyes, too.

"A baby? Oh, that's touching," Canales snapped. "And it works in my favor. You want your kid to live?"

It took Weston a moment to realize that Canales was talking to him. "Of course I want my baby and Addie to live. How can I make that happen?"

"Easy. I take Addie with me, and you'll help me undo all the damage she's done. It might include taking out a few FBI agents who can't be bribed. That idiot therapist, too."

Hell. Canales wanted him to murder to tie up all these loose ends.

"I can't trust you," Weston insisted. "How do I know you won't kill Addie the moment you leave here with her?"

"You don't. That's a chance you'll just have to take."

Addie was shaking her head, but it wasn't necessary. No way would Weston agree to a deal like that, because if Canales managed to get Addie out of here, there's no way he'd keep her alive.

"I'm Sheriff Lawton," someone called out. Backup. He was the sheriff from a neighboring town, and apparently Canales's thugs hadn't gotten to him.

Not yet anyway.

Weston hoped the sheriff had brought plenty of men with him.

"Marshal Seaver?" the sheriff added. "We got a problem out here."

"Yeah, we got a problem in here, too," Daniel answered. "A gunman with a hostage. What's going on out there?"

"There's a guy behind a tree, and he's armed with some kind of grenade-launcher-looking thing. He's got it aimed at the barn."

Not a grenade but a firebomb.

Daniel cursed. "Tell him not to pull the trigger. Tell him his boss is still alive in here."

That might stop the idiot from killing them all. But if he managed to shoot that firebomb into the rickety barn, their chances of surviving wouldn't be very good.

"Hank?" Canales called out, obviously speaking to his hired gun. "If I'm not out in one minute, launch that firebomb."

"But, boss, you'll die." It was easy to hear the hesitation in the man's voice.

"Yeah, but so will everybody else in here." Canales glared at Weston.

"You're bluffing," Weston snarled.

Canales laughed. "Either let me leave with Addie..." He stopped, shook his head in disgust. "You're not going to let me leave."

It wasn't a question, and in the same breath,

Canales shouted out to his hired gun. "Go ahead, Hank. Fire!"

There was no time to react. None. Weston heard the ominous sound. A split second later, the metal canister crashed through the front of the barn.

ADDIE TRIED TO shout for everyone to run, but she didn't get the chance to do or say anything.

Canales hooked his arm around her and, with her in tow, he leaped through the makeshift opening in the back of the barn. They immediately fell onto the ground, but thankfully, she didn't land on her stomach. Instead, she landed on the dead guy Ogden had shot just minutes earlier.

"Weston!" she yelled.

But she saw him before she even finished calling his name. He hurdled through the opening, landing right next to her.

Not a second too soon.

The flames and smoke swooshed out at them. The heat was blistering hot, but Weston saved her from being burned by scooping her up. He took off running. However, they weren't running alone.

Canales was right behind them.

The man came bolting out of the smoky cloud, his arms and legs pumping as fast as they could go.

"What about the marshals and Ogden?" she

managed to ask, though Addie wasn't sure how she could speak with so little breath.

"I think they got out through the front," Weston said.

*Think.* But he wasn't sure.

She prayed it was true, that they'd managed to get out in time. Even though Ogden had attempted to kill her several days ago, he'd also tried to save them tonight by shooting that hired gun Canales had brought with him. Or at least he'd appeared to save them. It was still possible Ogden was in on this.

Weston ran, but they'd only made it ten yards or so from the burning barn when Addie heard the gunshot. For one terrifying moment she thought Canales had shot Weston in the back, but then she realized that the sound had come from the front of the barn.

Had that hired thug managed to shoot Kirk or Daniel?

Addie didn't have time to figure that out, though, because she looked back and saw Canales had quit running.

He still had his gun.

"Stop or you die," Canales warned them. Not a shout, just a cold-blooded order that Addie knew they had no choice but to obey.

Weston pulled up, immediately releasing her

from his arms so that she was standing. And so that he was in front of her.

Protecting her again.

The problem was that Weston no longer had his gun. He'd likely dropped it in the earlier scuffle with Canales. And there really was no place for them to take cover. They were literally out in the open where Canales or one of his henchmen could gun them down.

"This is over," Weston told Canales. "Killing us now won't do anything except maybe add the death penalty to the charges you'll face."

"I'm already facing the death penalty," he admitted.

That was it, the only thing Canales said before he lifted his gun and took aim at them. He was no doubt about to pull the trigger when there was another sound.

A loud crash.

Behind him, the barn collapsed and sent a spray of smoke, debris and fire right at him. Canales glanced over his shoulder, cursed and started running again.

This time, right toward them.

And Weston was waiting for him.

"Get down," Weston told her.

He lunged right at Canales, tackling him, and like in the barn they went to the ground.

Weston didn't get hold of the gun, but he did

managed to grab Canales's right wrist, and he tried to wrench the gun away from him.

Canales held on.

Even when Weston bashed his hand against the ground.

Addie immediately looked around for something she could use to help. A rock or anything. But there was nothing. Just bits of the fiery debris from the barn, and Canales and Weston were rolling around, both of them jockeying for position.

The jockeying stopped with a gunshot.

The sound jolted through her and nearly brought her to her knees. Oh, God. Had Weston been hurt?

She couldn't tell, especially when the fight started again. Weston drew back his fist and punched Canales in the face, but the man must have been fueled with pure adrenaline because he was fighting like a wild animal.

Addie hurried closer to see if she could help, but she didn't get far when she saw Canales bring up his hand again. He still had hold of the gun, and he was trying to aim it at her.

She dropped back down to the ground.

Just as the shot blasted past her.

Weston glanced back at her. Cursing. And he punched Canales again. And again. Canales finally moved the gun so that it was no longer aimed at her.

But rather at Weston.

"Watch out," she warned Weston.

Though it was already too late for a warning. The sound of the shot tore through the night.

And the fight stopped.

Addie thought maybe her heart had, too.

She could only stay there for several terrifying moments. Moments where she didn't know if Weston was dead or alive. He wasn't moving. But then, neither was Canales.

"Weston?" she finally got out, and she forced her legs to move.

Addie went to Weston, caught him by the shoulder and moved him off Canales. That's when she saw the blood.

"I'm okay," Weston said to her.

It took her several more heart-stopping moments to realize it wasn't Weston's blood. It belonged to Canales, and it had covered the front of his shirt. Weston had hold of the man's gun.

Despite his injury, Canales laughed. "It's time for a deal."

"You're bleeding out," Weston told him. "Besides, you've got nothing I want."

"Maybe. But if I were you, I'd do everything possible to keep me alive."

"And why would I do that?" Weston asked.

Canales laughed again, but it was followed by a weak, shallow cough. "Because I know where the Moonlight Strangler is. I trapped him. And if you want him, then you'll make sure I'm a free man."

# *Chapter Twenty*

This ordeal wasn't over, but Weston hoped that it soon would be.

No thanks to Canales.

The man hadn't budged on telling them about the Moonlight Strangler before the ambulance had taken him away, but with some luck—or rather Jericho's interrogation skills—they might get the information from Canales's injured gunman, the one Daniel had shot. They'd gotten lucky that it wasn't a serious injury, so Jericho was with him at the hospital where he was being stitched up.

Weston didn't know the hired gun's name or what had caused him to get involved with a snake like Canales, but it didn't matter now. The only thing that mattered was his telling Jericho the location of the Moonlight Strangler. If there was a location to tell, that is. And if the thug wouldn't or couldn't tell them, then maybe Canales would do that when and if he came out of surgery.

The other thing that mattered, and it mattered

most, was that Addie and the baby were okay. For now. She still had that stunned look in her eyes. Still didn't seem too steady on her feet, which was why Weston had his arm around her.

That was one of the reasons anyway.

The other reason was because having her close steadied his own raw nerves.

"Canales could have been lying," Addie repeated, something both Weston and she had been reminding themselves of since they'd arrived at the sheriff's office to wait on news from Jericho. "We should be at the hospital to see if we can pressure the thug into talking."

Yes, that was tempting, and if Addie hadn't been in the picture, that's exactly where Weston would be. But it was still too big of a risk for Addie to be in the open. Actually, it was a risk for her to be anywhere, but at least he had Jax, Kirk and Daniel at the Appaloosa Pass sheriff's office to help guard her. Plus, the three lawmen were all working to track down some info on what was left of the investigation.

"I wish you'd sit down," Weston said to her—something else he'd been repeating for the past hour.

She looked up at him, their gazes connecting. "I'm still too wired."

It was the same for him. So, Weston tried a kiss instead. Just a quick brush of his mouth to hers.

Or at least that was the plan. But the kiss didn't stay quick. Weston added some pressure, pulled her closer to him until it finally helped. He felt Addie practically sag against him.

The kiss and the hug garnered Jax's attention, but her brother only gave a half smile and continued his phone conversation.

"Maybe we'll hear something about Ogden soon," she said.

Addie didn't have to add that she was worried about him. She was. So was Weston, but probably not worried in the same way as Addie. After all, the man had tried to kill Addie a few days ago, and he was no doubt insane. Even if he made a full recovery from his injuries, he'd spend the rest of his life in a mental hospital.

"Ogden did try to save us in the barn," Addie whispered.

He had indeed, and that was the only reason Weston didn't want to tear the man's head completely off. That and the fact that he was Addie's half-brother. However, that shared blood bond didn't extend to the Moonlight Strangler. Weston would kill him if he got the chance.

"SAPD picked up Boggs about a half hour ago," Jax said when he finished his latest call. "There won't be an arrest."

Not exactly a surprise. "Because of the statute of limitations on the gunrunning allegations," Weston said.

Jax nodded. "But at least Boggs is talking. He claims he only gave Canales money to fund the gunrunning, that he wasn't actually a part of it and that he wasn't part of the attacks, either."

"The cops believe him?" Addie asked.

Another nod from Jax. "There's nothing to link him to the attacks. Nothing to link him to anything that Canales did to get to Addie."

And Canales had done a lot. All because he'd been afraid that she might remember seeing him all those years ago.

"Boggs is ruined," Jax went on. "Even though he can't be charged with assorted felonies like Canales, if it's leaked to the press about his old connections to gunrunning, it'll cost him the campaign."

Good. That was something at least. Even if Boggs wasn't responsible for murder and attempted murder, he didn't deserve to hold political office.

"You okay?" Jax asked, his gaze nailed to Addie.

"No, she's not," Weston answered for her. "I'm taking her to the break room." There was a cot back there, and maybe she could get some rest.

"I'm okay, really," she insisted.

That was partly true. The medic had checked

her out right after they'd arrived at the sheriff's office, and at least she hadn't physically been harmed. Mentally was a whole different story, but she dug in her heels to stay put.

"Convince me you're okay," Weston challenged.

She kissed him. Since he'd done the same to her just seconds earlier, he figured she'd gotten the idea from him. It was a nice distraction. Nice for his body, too, to feel that heat slide through him.

"Not very convincing," he grumbled.

Addie lifted her eyebrow. "Really?"

"The kiss doesn't prove you're okay. It just proves we're attracted to each other. We already knew that."

The eyebrow lift continued.

"Okay, more than just attracted," Weston admitted.

A whole lot more that he would have told her if Jax's phone hadn't rang.

"Jericho," Jax greeted when he answered the call.

That stopped Weston, and both Addie and he went back to Jax's desk so they could hear what Jericho had to say. Jax put the call on speaker for them.

"Canales died in surgery," Jericho started. "But the rat he hired started talking when I mentioned the death penalty was on the table. According to the rat, Canales lured the Moonlight Strangler to

Daisy's house. I've got the county sheriff on his way there now, and yeah, he's taking plenty of backup with him. They'll be out there any minute now."

The county sheriff would need all the help he could get if he did indeed come face-to-face with the killer.

"Why lure him to Daisy's place?" Weston wanted to know.

"Apparently, Canales persuaded the killer that there was a photo at Daisy's that he needed to retrieve. A photo that would reveal his identity."

Addie pulled in a sharp breath. "We need to find that photo."

"Doesn't exist," Jericho explained. "According to the rat, it was just a lure to get the Strangler there so two more of Canales's hired guns could capture him. That way, Canales would look like the big hero, and that in turn would be some good publicity for the campaign."

Weston thought about that for a moment. Not a bad plan, but things had clearly gone to hell in a hand basket. However, he had the feeling this was more than just a campaign ploy. "If there was a connection between Canales, the Moonlight Strangler and the gunrunning, then Canales would want the Strangler dead so the connection couldn't come back to bite him."

"That's my best guess, too," Jericho agreed. "I

can't think of another reason Canales would go to all that trouble to lure a killer there."

Neither could Weston. "Call me when you hear anything from the county sheriff."

"Will do. And you'd better take good care of my sister," Jericho added before he ended the call.

It wasn't a surprising request, but there was something in Jericho's voice. Not exactly a warning but more like a strong suggestion.

Or maybe Weston was reading what he wanted to read into it.

And what he wanted to read into it was that he did indeed want to take care of Addie. Not just because of the danger. And not just for tonight.

Weston realized he wanted a whole lot more.

"What?" Addie asked, staring at him.

Probably because he had a strange look on his face. The look of a man who'd just been thunderstruck.

Well, heck.

"When did this happen?" Weston had intended to keep that question in his head, but it somehow made it out of his mouth.

Addie kept staring. "When did what happen?" The last word sort of died on her lips though, and she shook her head. "No, you're not going to ask me to marry you."

Since that's exactly what he'd planned to do, Weston was sure he looked even more thunderstruck than before. He was also a little riled that Addie seemed riled.

"Why not?" Weston demanded.

Then he realized something else. The three lawmen in the squad room were no longer on their phones. They were listening to him fumbling around. And they were somewhat amused by it. Even Jax. Of course, he could be amused because Addie had just shot Weston down.

Or not.

"You giving up that easy?" Jax asked. "My advice, don't. You two belong together. More advice—finish this conversation in the break room." He tipped his head in that direction.

It seemed to be an endorsement from her brother. One that Weston didn't need, but was still thankful for. He couldn't say the same for Addie.

"Stay out of this," she warned Jax, and she no longer sounded exhausted and shaky.

"No," Addie continued once they made it to the break room. She whirled around to face him. "You're not going to propose to me simply because you're blaming yourself for the danger I was in. Or because you're relieved we're alive. Or because I'm pregnant with—"

Weston kissed her again. It was meant to distract her. And it worked.

Of course, it distracted him, too. Addie's mouth

had a way of doing that to him. Ditto for the rest of her.

When they were both good and breathless, Weston broke the kiss and looked down at her. "What if I'm not asking for any of those reasons?"

She blinked, probably because she hadn't been expecting that. Or the knock that caused her to gasp. The door wasn't closed, but Jax had knocked on the frame to get their attention.

"Sorry to interrupt." Jax held up his phone.

Weston cursed but then remembered Jax wouldn't have come back here if it weren't important.

"Two things." Jax paused as if debating which news to give them first.

"Something happened?" Addie asked, touching her fingers to her mouth.

"Everyone's okay," her brother reassured her. "Well, everyone who counts. Ogden is out of surgery and will soon be on the way to a state mental hospital. He wanted to give you a message, though. He says he's sorry."

While that seemed to soothe Addie a little, both Weston and she were waiting for the other boot to drop.

"The county sheriff didn't catch the Moonlight Strangler," Weston tossed out.

"No, he didn't," Jax verified. "But the killer was at Daisy's house. At least it looks that way. Both of Canales's hired guns are dead. Both strangled and their faces cut."

The same MO as the Moonlight Strangler.

Since the face cut wasn't common knowledge, it was their proof that her birth father had indeed been there.

Jax came closer and held his phone out for Addie to see. "The Strangler left you a handwritten message."

Weston's instinct was to step in front of her, to protect her from reading whatever the killer had left for her. She'd already been through way too much tonight to have more added to her burden. But there was no way he could stop her, of course.

"Addie, I was never after you and yours," she read aloud. "Never will be. That was Canales playing games, and he paid for it. Blood ties are worth something to me. Be happy."

It wasn't a scrawled message but rather neatly written on a plain piece of paper.

"You all right?" Jax asked her.

Addie nodded. Cleared her throat and nodded again. "It's really from him. He means it. He won't be coming after us."

"Maybe. It could be a fake," Jax argued.

"No," she argued back. Though she didn't elaborate, Weston could tell she felt, in her gut, that she was safe from her birth father.

He felt it, too.

"The note will be processed for prints and trace," Jax added.

Weston doubted they'd find anything. The Moonlight Strangler had almost certainly taken precautions. And while Weston still hated the man to his core, he was thankful that he'd given Addie this small measure of peace.

Weston felt that same sense of peace. Finally. Addie and his baby would be safe.

"Guess there's no reason for you two to hang around here," Jax said. He shifted his gaze to Weston. "Why don't you go ahead and take Addie home...after you've finished your proposal."

Jax was probably attempting to lighten things up a little. He failed. Well, kind of. The somber mood was still there, hanging over them, but for the first time in days there was the hope of something good. Something right.

"Will you marry me?" Weston asked, and he kissed her again, hoping it would cloud her mind enough for her to jump right into saying yes.

It didn't work.

Another "no" left her mouth when they broke for air. "There's only one reason I'll ever marry, and it's not because I'm pregnant."

Oh.

That.

Well, shoot. Weston regrouped. "I thought it was obvious. I'm in love with you."

"Obvious, yes. But you still have to say it."

Weston smiled. "I love you." And just in case she hadn't caught it, he repeated it a couple more times in between kisses. "And now I want the words, too. Give them to me, Addie."

She pulled back, ran her tongue over her bottom lip. A little gesture that had his body begging for a yes and a whole lot more. But first, he wanted that yes.

"Well?" he prompted.

Addie fought a smile. "Convince me that this is exactly what you want, that you're really in love with me."

"Convince you?" he repeated. "I think I've heard that expression somewhere before."

"The man I love says it a lot. But this time, I want more than words. Convince me, Weston."

He did exactly that. He convinced Addie the best way he knew how. Weston pulled Addie to him and kissed her.

* * * * *